BUILI

UNIVERSES

Ileana Stoica, PhD

En Passant

europe books

www.europebooks.co.uk | info@europebooks.co.uk

ISBN 9791256972449
First edition February 2026

The book cover idea, images and realisation belong to the author.
For more information, contact: ileana@scilogism.com

DISCLAIMER

While inspired by true stories, this book is largely a work of fiction. Characters, places, businesses, incidents and dialogues have been changed substantially, and some are the product of the author's imagination.

En Passant

To the unlikely heroes who live to fight another day

My thanks go to my family, friends and beta-readers
for their patient and thorough feedback.
I wish to gratefully acknowledge the support
provided by the editorial team at Europe Books.

Table of Contents

Chapter 1.
"Evening Walks Are Good for Health"

David closed the door behind him and walked quietly back to his desk. Around him, people were hiding behind their computers, typing away, almost merging with their screens. "What do humans do when they can't use their fight or flight response? They freeze." His mother had said this once – where was she reading all that stuff? Only this time, it seemed to David that his colleagues had found a new response: flight *and* freeze. They looked like an army of desperate yet disciplined robots, locked in a state of lifeless busyness. "Good for them," thought David, "but this cannot be me. I've got to face reality head-on: I'd just been let go from my job. And so will the entire bunch, one by one, no matter how frantically they are hitting their keyboards, glued to their seats as if it still means anything to anyone." On every Quant's computer screen, the graphs and data looked the same: lifeless. Soon, all the charts would point to the abyss. It was an all-around collapse – not just of trends and data, but of the system as a whole. No conceivable development in the world of capital markets was going to halt it. Two floors up, the traders were a little more tuned into the big picture, but it did not take an Einstein to understand this was the end of financial modelling as they knew it.

If he was being honest, David was surprised it took so long to get there. The inevitability of the disaster had become clearer with each passing day, ever since the Lehman Brothers' bankruptcy in September. The financial giants were crumbling down, one after another, in a grim fairy tale. A tale the media was quick to infuse with schadenfreude disguised as self-righteousness. It was the tale of greedy people getting their comeuppance – except that lots of innocent people were punished in the process too. It had taken a couple of months for the British financial market to hit rock bottom, but, of course, it eventually did in December. That the London team – David's team – had been allowed a relatively peaceful Christmas holiday was unusual. Maybe employment laws in Britain were less ruthless than in North America. Yet, here he was, getting kicked out – on Valentine's Day of all days. He was given the customary one-month notice and was advised, politely but firmly, to make use of all his accrued holidays so he'd be out the door in twenty days at most. The London office had to wind down the entire Quantitative Analysis operation – that's how he knew all his colleagues were getting the boot, too, and soon – and time was of the essence.

Outside David's window in the office, the shadows of the trees were dim and elongated like a bunch of droopy theatre masks. A streetlamp started flickering across the street. It was four o'clock. David figured this was a perfectly reasonable time to make his way out of the office. Now that he'd been laid off, presenteeism was no longer necessary. He went into the kitchen to wash his tea mug, then came back to his desk and started tidying up some papers. All in slow motion – what was the point of rushing? He pondered for a second whether he should save any of his files on a USB stick. Surely, this was against the law. But, barring the company-sensitive data, he had a few personal files, such as his work permit issued in Canada, a couple of annual Human Resource appraisals, and, of course, his up-to-date CV. Not that he'd get to use it any time soon. David was fully aware he was sinking – and, along with him, an entire sector of the economy. Once vibrant, with tens of thousands of people in its employment, financial services now had the vitality of a corpse. In all fairness, it was part deserved – the media and pop psychology were not entirely wrong. There had been inexcusable excesses; he only had to listen to his trader friends boasting about their bonuses to know some of the stories were true enough. As for himself, David had only graduated three years ago, of which two and a half were spent in Finance. He'd hardly had the time to make the kind of money that corrupted. Besides, the Quants were data nerds. They were not rewarded handsomely since they did not bring in any new business and did not make any measurable profits. Quants had a supporting role on the big set that was life in Finance; the limelight was always on the Trading floor. Speaking of limelight, David could not help observing how Clarissa, who was standing next to her desk but staring intently in his direction, was looking more agitated than usual. Wherever she went, Clarissa captured the light around her. She had the most luminous eyes David had ever seen in a human being, and the most ethereal appearance. Well, that was it for seeing Clarissa every day, talking to her during coffee breaks, laughing together … dreaming that one day she might become his girl. Just as he was about to log off for the day, he noticed one new email: "Happy Valentine, David! Meet me in front of the building at five."

He was done by four forty-five and could not bear one more minute in that stuffy office. A zoo packed with ostriches; that's how it looked like to him. Time to get his head out of the sand, breathe the air, face the music, whatever it might be. Outside, the darkness was forgiving and the evening mild – the perks of winter in London. Well, soon that would be over too. Back to Montréal's harsh, icy, bright and endless winters! For now, he had to wait for Clarissa; he'd promised. He lit up a cigarette and patiently stood in front of the entrance. His gaze was distracted by a flock of noisy birds in the dark sky, flying away orderly towards friendlier climates. "Dark swans," smiled David bitterly, "they've reached our skies eventually. I wonder how those Dutch mariners must have felt hundreds of years ago, seeing black swans for the first time on landing in Australia? Until then, black swans were merely symbolic, a bad omen that was feared but never really came to happen. I don't know about them, but I know how *I* feel: relieved we're finally facing the big black swan who's taking us, and the stock markets, on the ride of a lifetime. We're going to hit the collective rock bottom. But from here, as Dad would say, the only way is up."

A couple of young women from the Accounts stopped to look at him as they were making their way out, then walked on, chuckling. What a nosey species, these people were … what was the special interest in him and his pathetic date – if he could even call it that way? He had no business complaining too much about Britain though. After all, David had chosen London right out of grad school. Compared with New York – the other big hub where young people like him could hope to set a foot in the industry door – London seemed more toned down and closer to his sensibilities. Even the famous British stiff upper lip, which was real enough, was fine for David – he too liked to keep things inside sometimes, put on a brave face and calmly carry on. Since all roads in London led to finance, soon after his arrival he'd found himself interviewing for hedge funds, financial consultancies, and later, the big banks. Job hunting had been smooth enough for David, though Britain was never a place he fathomed as his home. This was a passionless love affair, but one that gave him a sense of stability and groundedness he could not find in the US, with its overt competitiveness and arrogance. He'd seen glimpses of this world while studying at Yale and did not wish to join it once he completed his degree. London was duller perhaps, not so dynamic, but he enjoyed the lesser pressure. He'd been promoted to Senior Quant after only two years without having to jockey for the position. David had done surprisingly well in his role – until now, of course. Although, if he was being honest with himself, most of the time he was just going through the motions, keeping his distance – just like his colleagues. Except for Clarissa. She seemed to have a different emotional register from the rest, and more intrigue to her. Everyday life did not appear to bore Clarissa: where did she get her drama from? It must have been something from inside, David was certain. Something he may have shared as well but was afraid to let it come to surface. An inarticulate yearning for intensity. Well, with the Financial Crash, the lack of drama had stopped being a problem, and his attraction for Clarissa had been subsiding lately. Besides, she seemed physically shy, a little frigid. Nobody really knew, with women, anyway …

True to her word, Clarissa appeared at five on the dot. "I thought you stood me up!" she said in a weepy voice. Clarissa was never *not* sad, even when she was happy. He knew she was happy and content when she was with him, but cheerfulness – that was not part of her emotional repertoire. A regretful happiness was the most this girl could summon. Who was he kidding? He still found her magnetic. He'd never meet another Clarissa, that he could be sure of. "Stand you up? I don't do this kind of thing. Not to friends, not to anyone." He put off the cigarette. "Where to?" he asked, wanting to sound confident and taking her arm gently. She did not pull away; she seemed pleased to be leaning on him. "Anywhere, as long as we get to walk together. Evening walks are good for health. Sloane Square! That's where I live, anyway." "Wowser, I did not think people actually *lived* there." "I'm not just any people, you know," she teased. She often acted flirty with him – and others – in a rather generic, scripted way. "Actually, the apartment was an inheritance. It came when I least expected it, five years ago. My grandmother … she passed away." "Oh … sorry to hear that," said David. "Well, she was old … she was my only family, in fact. My parents got killed in a car accident when I was eight." David stopped walking and instantly let go of her arm. She'd never mentioned anything during their innumerable conversations, brief and not so brief, over the past year. He was stunned to hear such an intimate story so abruptly. But if not now, when? A faint drizzle started falling from the dense clouds above. Under the streetlamp, he could see the glimmer of water droplets spreading onto Clarissa's hair and coat. He could also see her tears. "I don't know why I'm telling this to you of all people, but I've always had the feeling that I can talk to you, and you to me," added Clarissa, almost whispering. She pulled him back towards her, as if losing his proximity was not an option. Reluctantly, David resumed the walking, his hand now held tightly by her hand. "That's ok. I do not think you chose me accidentally. I'm here if you need to get things off your chest. But I should tell you something too. We're getting sacked, Clarissa … all of us, the entire team … the floor. I was just told today. I am not sure why they picked me first, maybe because I am Canadian. My work permit is tied to this employer, so they had to give me time to act. And even it wasn't so abrupt … sooner or later I would have made my way home. You know, the real home. I could not face another year in this place … alone." "But you are not alone!" Clarissa's weepy voice turned loud and shrill. "You cannot go! You didn't even ask me … I am not giving my permission!"

She turned around, blocking the sidewalk, standing in his way. Her eyes had changed completely; they had become opaque and dark, and unforgiving. "It isn't like I wished for it, Clarissa … You actually look like you hate me right now, you know that? And there's no point, really …" "No point? No point in what? You did want it, admit it, David – at the back of your mind, you've been hating this office, this country, and me, all along. You didn't want to give the two of us a chance!" "I've never known there was an us! I mean, I've had girlfriends at Yale, they'd always let me know … they were straightforward about it, and it was ok. You've had over a year and all we did was flirt like teenagers: me hoping, and then … nothing. This kind of push and pull is just not …" "Not what? Say it, David – not healthy? Not healthy enough for you?" "I didn't say that word – you did. I like you – I more than like you, all right? But I'll be going my way. It's time. Look at the mess this world is in! I just wanted to warn you of what's about to happen, and otherwise … say my good-bye." David stopped; he'd said enough. It was as civilised a way out as he could find. He did feel sorry for her – he always did – but also kind of scared. He did not have the time for another thought as he felt Clarissa's body pressing onto him, pushing his back against the iron gate. An apartment building was behind them – quite possibly her own apartment building. Her breath was heavy. The ethereal girl – whom he had imagined a bit frigid all this time – was now, suddenly, all fire. She cupped his head into her hands and kissed him, a long kiss. Then she slid down her hand, rubbing against him, gently at first, then harder, and then unclasped his belt. She whispered in a raspy voice, pacing her words to match her strokes: "So, you were hoping, thinking about me all along? Were you ever hoping for this? Did you imagine I could be the most amazing, thrilling sex of your life?" "No … no … hell, no!" His whole body shuddered, and he grabbed her hand, stopping her at the last moment. He felt painfully aroused and just as painfully demeaned. "Not like that … I don't want you like that. I told you I was leaving … I'm telling you now to stay away!" "Or else …what?" Clarissa's beautiful features had morphed into a grimace; her mouth was tensed, reduced to a line. Her long hair was wet and dangling, her glare was stinging and malicious. He stepped back, horrified – but it was Clarissa who acted out the outrage. Not just an act; with no mind of her own, she had become a perfect, upside-down mirror to his mind. "You're not healthy, David!" she screamed as she was rummaging in her purse for the keys. "You need to talk to someone – not me!"

***

That night he could not close his eyes for a second. The pit of his stomach was painfully contracted at all times, whilst his limbs were listless and his head throbbing. At last, David decided to get going for the day. He put his head under the water tap, letting the cold stream run over his hair and eyes. It didn't work. He was still moving slowly, in a haze, watching his own moves as if he watched a film. Scene one, David wakes up and makes his coffee. The painful lump in his throat does not allow him to drink it, so he leaves the cup on the table. Scene two, he puts on his suit. No, not the trousers he was wearing last night. Those ones … those ones go into the bin. Shame, the suit had cost Dad five hundred Canadian dollars; they'd gone together to the best tailor in downtown Montréal to have it fit. "This is your first grown-up suit, Davidutz. I hope it brings you luck!" He remembered Codrin's eyes tearing up for a split second. It did bring him luck – for a while. Now … now he was moving on to scene number three: switch on the TV, listen to the latest gloom and doom. "The Financial Crisis is here to stay. The Stock Market is worth half of what it was this time last year. Chancellor asked to resign amid market turmoil. Young analyst tragically jumps off Goldman Sacks' 8th floor." Enough! Stop feeding on people's pain, media leeches! The lump of tears in his throat was mounting higher, and David finally broke down. "*Eli, Eli, lama sabachthani?* Why did you desert that young guy in his darkest hour? His parents – how are they going to live for the rest of their lives, day after day after day, after this? And for what? What is this city other than a disgusting Vanity Fair in Your eyes?"

He was about an hour late for work. Just as well; what were they going to do – fire him? As he came in, David noticed the commotion about the open-plan office. Around him, people showed split reactions: some hid behind their screens like they always did, others were looking straight towards him with dismay. And yet others – a very small group – had a strange, knowing look. Clarissa was pacing up and down in front of the main meeting room, where all the important news was delivered; in David's case, his layoff the day before. At first, he thought she too had been laid off, as he'd predicted – until he saw the look of jubilation on her face. What had she done?

He was greeted by a non-descript young girl from HR: "This way, David – get inside, please. You are not to go to your desk today or talk to anyone, do you understand?" He reckoned he'd copied the wrong file on his USB stick and was prepared to hand it over for inspection, when the HR assistant took his arm and almost shoved him inside the room. What gave this small woman the right to handle him that way? Why did these people feel justified to get physical with him all of a sudden?

Once inside the room, he took a seat. “Yes, you may sit down,” the woman added. He had not asked for her permission and did not thank her. The atmosphere was beyond hostile this morning – but why? He’d taken the redundancy well, with no protests or discussions. His severance package was minimal but, as a mid-level Quant, David knew he couldn’t do much better, so he did not even bother to complain. If he was being honest, he could not wait for the whole circus to be over. He was so lucky to have people at home waiting for him, ready to have him back, not only with no questions asked, but with their arms wide open. “Now, David, your colleague has told us everything that happened last night. We understand you were upset and troubled by the news, but you had no reason to take it out on her like that.” “Take out? Me … on whom?” “The fact that you’re pretending you don’t understand tells us all we need to know. Clarissa, of course. She’s put it all in writing. Not only that, but she is formally accusing you of stalking and assault.” “Of what? … No way, that’s not what happened at all! If anything, I mean, I wouldn’t normally go as far as that, but this time … I could say it was the other way around.” “And you expect us to believe you – as women, as professionals? Is that what you were taught in the Ivy League? To turn the tables around on a woman like that, and go on the offensive?” “I didn’t mean to come across as aggressive, sorry. If you show me her letter, I could pick her claims point by point and tell you what really happened.” “Of course, we’re not allowed to show you that letter – you do know that's company policy, right? We can, however, give you a piece of paper to write down your own version of events. As I am sure you're aware, in our organisation we take these accusations very seriously indeed." "You mean, allegations?" "Whatever. We need from you every single detail of what happened last night, from 5 PM to 7 PM. Actually, not 5 PM but 4.45 – two of your office mates saw you stalking the office building; waiting for her, no doubt." "*She* emailed me, set up a date … and then she … look, I'll write down as much as I can remember." "Surely, you do remember all of it if you're as innocent as you say?" "Yeah, well, for some reason, I woke up with a massive brain fog today. I may not be able to detail every single minute, but I can give you a full account nonetheless. First of all, the layoff did not have the effect you are describing. I felt quite calm, relieved even. But once we were outside, Clarissa and me, it was dark and confusing … she is a very confusing woman. Her actions contradict themselves; they don't make sense. It is as if she's …" "You are not being asked to give your opinion on your colleague's personality, David. Just write things down … to the best of your memory, of course." Her tone was ironic. And cruel. She was a nobody in the company; he did not even remember her name. She was about to get fired too in a few weeks' time; they just needed her around for a bit longer until the layoffs were completed. But there was more: David got the distinct impression there was something about Clarissa that she – they – knew, and not just the HR, but a few people in the office too. It was as if they'd almost expected this development, though nobody was about to acknowledge it out loud. "It is because I am the foreigner," he thought. "Not one of them. Cannot be trusted, cannot be told. It's something they're embarrassed of, it would seem."

Alone in the room, he wrote a few lines, then put the pencil down. Clarissa's gesture had astounded him, but her euphoric mood after the fact was not just viscerally hurtful – it was incomprehensible. What had he done but be nice to her? Where was his fault last night, the turning point? That he was leaving – *her*? Is that how she perceived the situation – so personal and so mistaken? She certainly reacted as if they had been married for the past year. Not one bit of information about the company, redundancies, Recession had entered her mind, so frenzied was she in declaring war on him. But even so, how could she? "Is this what people call betrayal? This punch right in the stomach, immobilising, sickening? Is this how life's supposed to be? *Eli, Eli …*" David tried hard to stop his thoughts and write down the rest of the episode, but he had lost his focus. He kept remembering the young man in the news. Bloodhounds, the lot of them! His eyes were tired and teary. Good that at least there was no one around to see him. So pointless … such an uncaring, stupid crowd. "Outside, the world is going mad, and all they care about are the ravings of a fragile mind. There is also the sex … or rather, the lack of it," he followed on with bitterness. "Do these people get any? They sure have a disproportionate preoccupation with the topic. Do they even understand how other people work, other than by watching 'Coronation Street' or some soap opera that could not be missed on TV, at seven on the dot every evening? Did they ever get to see the world beyond their doorstep? Not much of it, judging by their need to trigger oversized reactions in people just because they were unable to read the smaller, subtler ones. When someone needs to hurt others as a tool to probe the workings of their mind, you know that person is defective. I am not perfect either, but this time I got caught in the middle of a deeply dysfunctional bunch." Two hours passed. He was done writing. He had left out the juicy stuff on purpose, denying them the titillating pleasure – also because, to his surprise, the details were still hazy in his mind. Especially the screaming and shoving coupled with touching and whispering and … well, his attraction for Clarissa. Man, was she twisted for doing this to him!

Lunch time came and he heard people moving outside. How come they could afford to keep this room just for him – where were they doing the layoffs today? Ah, the small meeting room, surely. The whole thing was absurd, pathetic, a soap opera plot gone awry. He opened the door. "Where are you going, David?" Incredibly, the HR assistant was still outside. They'd given her a tiny desk and a chair right next to the door. She was effectively his prison guard. "Here is the testimonial. And, erm, I need to use the bathroom … please." "You cannot do that, I'm afraid." "It's lunch break, can't I go get lunch?" "No; sorry. Not until you are cleared of the charges." He went back inside and closed the door. "These people are capable of calling the police." He needed to pee – badly. In a flash, he was taken back to one time in kindergarten when he could barely hold it. He must have been around five. "What you do, David," his mum trained him at home, "is you picture something completely different. Like your toy chess pieces. You then arrange them on the board like Dad taught you to, slowly, and then you scramble them. And re-arrange them back, carefully. And again. You'll never know when class is over and you hear the bell ring." He lowered the blinds; he could do anything since they'd left him alone in the room. He rose from his chair and sat down on the carpet, in the corner, under the window … then he lay down. It was dark and quiet now, and he was feeling drained. Last night's lack of sleep caught up with him.

When he woke up, the clock in the room showed 4 o'clock. That was it; he'd given them enough excitement for one day. They needed to go back to their lousy layoffs. He opened the door again. "I thought I told you, David, that you can't …" "Fuck off," he said loudly, without as much as looking her way, and went straight to the bathroom.

In the days that followed, nobody from the office summoned him back. What a relief! David found it impossible to imagine seeing their faces again after their parting shot. No friend or colleague called him either. If a police case was ever opened, he was not contacted about it. A single letter came in the post, from the HR. One paragraph informing him that, in light of the "grave accusations" that had been brought against him, he was dismissed with immediate effect. A final payslip was included, for two weeks' time until the end of February – they had removed his holiday allowance. This meant that David was running out of money, and fast. He called up Mr. Anoum, his landlord. Mr. Anoum's daughter, who had been laid off in December and was now doing legal work for her dad's property business, proposed a deal: David would vacate the apartment by mid-March and the landlord would forget about the two-month notice in their contract. "You don't look too good, son," the man observed as they were signing the papers. "I came to London on my own as well, some thirty years ago. Whoever tells you it's a lot of fun … is full of it. If you don't have to work – perhaps. But not for me, it wasn't. Better have some rest if you can; that's what I tell my daughter too. I never did."

Chapter 2. Ashen

For weeks on end, sleeping in his old room on Rue Lemieux was unbearable for David. To his parents, he blamed it on the jet lag – but he knew better. He was alone. No, strike that; he was surrounded by people who loved him – but he felt oh-so-lonely in his grief! The numbness that had set during his last weeks in London was eroding, and he was finally feeling something: a shapeless pain. Hour after hour, it swept over him, dragging him deeper into the night without a hint of comeback. A sense of desolation and unravelling burst out somatically, taking root in his insomnia. Back to familiar surroundings, his body was finally safe to react. On a rational level, David knew it was a luxury to be afforded a reaction at all – but, in the moment, it struck him as a torture. His restless journey through the night felt like a brutal rite of passage, a stubborn reckoning with a reality that never gave him peace. As darkness fell, a tired but wired state made it impossible for David to lie down on his own bed. He would then pace around, glancing outside the window at the dimming lights and empty streets. Soon, his own experience with dim lights and empty streets in London came back, raw, sending a shot of pain right through his solar plexus. To banish it, he would climb down into the kitchen to get a glass of milk – his childhood habit. It didn't work to calm him. Compulsively and cyclically, his mind would run through past events, rewinding dialogues, expressions, reactions, searching for cues and explanations – anything to reconcile the absurdity of those days. Not knowing any better, his brain – this exquisite but automatic machine that takes over when we are overwhelmed – re-lived each episode with the same searing humiliation at the injustice of it all. As the night passed, this fury-fuelled drama transmuted into a harrowing, tearless sorrow, which he felt even less equipped to deal with than the anger. Both brain and heart were wounded; nothing was ever reconciled or healed. Exhausted and defeated, afraid he'd been irreparably damaged in some way, David would finally lie down. A toxic fatigue diffused throughout his body, like ink shot by an ill-meaning octopus. He'd lift his pillow slightly so he could catch the ashen dawn over the park at Plamondon. In the uncanny stillness of the early morning, he could make out the silhouettes of the first joggers starting their daily routine, overseen from afar by L'Oratoire St. Joseph. "Maniacs!" he'd mumble, with a mix of irritation and relief at seeing other human beings. Then and only then would David give himself permission to surrender to sleep. It was as if he had been waiting all night for confirmation that he was indeed at odds with all the world, and was alone in that.

The first month was spent trapped inside, oblivious to everything around him. Here he was, a voluntary prisoner of his home and mind. Outside, under the fickle April sun, the snow over the streets, benches and trees had started thawing. Underneath it, the garbage that piled up over the winter months was left exposed and uncollected. He'd never noticed this passing of the seasons while in London, as there was never any snow to fall and then to melt. Besides, in London, David was constantly rushing from one place to another, taking the underground everywhere. He likened his underground rides to crossing the River Styx to shadow land. "Shadows indeed … a bleak show of make-believe, is what this was. Nothing was as it seemed; they were all fake. *She* was all fake – deliberately so." Now, finally, something inside him was thawing after the London chapter. What surfaced was old stuff, unclaimed, just like the mess outside. It was the dormant, fractured, ashen landscape of his heart.

"The key to healing can be found in words." Who spoke just now? He'd finally managed to doze off for an hour after a sleepless night, when he was woken by a whisper, soft but clear, right next to him. Words – David had never trusted words much. He preferred facts, proofs, tactics. But if he was to give it a try, this was the time. Slowly, he sought and found the language to describe his pain, bringing it out in the open, making sense out of nonsense. So, what hurt? Losing his job was bad enough with its inevitable sense of failure, but that was just the tip of the iceberg. That evening with Clarissa had activated his visceral understanding of how dangerously thin the boundaries between human beings could be. The monstrosity of her euphoria after the fact had shown him that human loyalty was just as precarious a concept. And finally, *that* day in the office. He'd seen the tables turned and facts conveniently spun around, simply by virtue of "several" uniting against "one" – the outsider; the one presumed guilty; in this instance, David. It was not normal to be kept alone and locked inside a room for a whole day; hungry, thirsty, needing to pee. He could articulate that now, but back then it was all a blur. That might have been the purpose of Clarissa's letter – her attack – to catch him unaware and unprepared. Not just Clarissa, though: the whole HR crew seemed perversely at ease dealing with him confused and on the defence, half of his brain shut off in shock. It wasn't until he took distance and started living among sane people again, that he was able to recapture a minimal degree of certainty about those facts and people. That normalcy was now restored and unconditionally available to him filled

David with a wave of gratitude. He owed it to his parents – and yet he found himself unable to say a single word to them about what happened.

In fact, during those first few weeks, David could not look his father in the eye. But curiously, the disappointment he expected from Codrin on his return was not there – not one fleeting expression, frown or sigh. In fact, one day, to break the tension, Codrin told him to his face: “David, you are a grown-up now. If you wish to punish yourself for whatever you think you’ve done, go right ahead. Just don’t ask me to side with the world and against you. I haven’t done this in 28 years since we’ve had you, I am not about to start it now.” “Besides, just look around you,” his mum jumped in. That was the first annoying thing about those two: their interventions – rare but always in tandem, reinforcing each other. The second thing was that they were … how were they? “Supportive” was not the word … *adoring*. They couldn’t get enough of him, could see no wrong in him. It made it hard for David to make any mistake and even harder to say a word about it, lest he might fall off their pedestal. Undisturbed, Rada continued her argument: “Yeah, look around … even Québec is feeling the recoil, and God knows our finance sector is all but non-existent. The markets are crashing down around us; it would be madness to persist finding a job in finance – or in London. Why knock on closed doors? You’ve been so smart to come home! The three of us, we’re smarter than the rest – and you know why? Because we choose not to shoot ourselves in the foot – *that* is what being Jewish means to me. Why go along with the rest of the world, with its warped thinking and ego trips, and feel embarrassed to be a member of the club who wants you? We want you, and I am sure we’re not the only ones. And also, who says you have to hop from one job to another? We are comfortable financially – think of all the money you've saved us over the years by not going to a private school. I should know – I've pored over our finances for evenings on end, not quite believing we were actually doing well. And then, your scholarship at Yale. *That!* Now that was years' worth of savings, way more than some mindless job in this disastrous economy."

Rada poured herself more tea. They were seated, all three of them, around a small round table, Rada's favourite, which she had awkwardly fit against the corner of their living room. Behind the table, in the tiny triangle between the walls, stood his mother's old floor lamp, brought over from her childhood home, which was just a few streets away in the middle of the Orthodox Jewish community. She'd also brought with her a samovar. Nobody knew exactly how the family had acquired those objects, but Rada loved them ever since she was a little girl. She had an attachment to all things Russian, which was strange because nobody in her family was Russian – that she knew of. Besides, her relationship with her Jewishness was even stranger.

As she sipped her tea, Rada made sure her moves were slow and small. Despite the years spent apart, his mum was still an open book: she had let her passion take over, as always when talking to David, and now decided to keep herself in check. For all her larger-than-life feelings, Rada took most pride in her analytical side. In the silent minutes that followed, his father saw an opening and made a suggestion: "There might be one thing if you are really getting bored. They're asking me at my CEGEP if I know a chess coach. Apparently, chess is back in fashion nowadays. It must have something to do with computers: we had Kasparov against Deep Blue in the 90's, then Kramnik against Deep Fritz just a few years ago. Kids see these stories in the news and don't just want to beat each other – they want to take on the machines!" His father's enthusiasm was too much for David. Staring down into his tea, he snapped: "That is for losers, Dad. You know I'm out." He was half-lying; while in Britain, he had continued playing chess for clubs, with good results. Why did he need to be harsh with his old man? David knew Codrin was sensitive about one thing and one thing only: feeling rejected by him or Rada. Was he being antagonistic on purpose, in a roundabout attempt to air his troubles? Was it because his tea companions were the only people in the world who cared about him, and thus safe to bear the brunt of his ordeal? Whatever it was, it had an immediate effect. Codrin never brought up the subject again, and tea around the samovar happened less and less. Besides, no amount of tea and biscuits in the world could take away the ashen taste in David's mouth.

***

David was not prone to introspection; that was his mother's skill. But they did have one big thing in common: dreaming. Dreams were the stuff their bond was made of. One night, when he was eight or nine, David came running into his parents' bedroom and shook his mother's arm to wake her up. Tears were streaming down his face. "What is it, baby, what happened?" whispered Rada. They went to David's bedroom, holding hands. "Mummy … I know something. I am *loved*!" Rada's expression was transfixed, gripped by a great awe. "It wasn't a bad dream … it was a good one, wasn't it? A very, very good dream?" David shook his head.

They sat on the bed together as if under a common spell. "Who did you see? A man, a woman?" "A woman." "Middle-aged, ordinary looking, with a shawl around her shoulders?" "She didn't have a shawl. She had grey hair though. And she was very, very kind." "How did you know she was kind?" "I just knew. We didn't speak." "Where were you? Alone in an old, foreign city with a large plaza?" David nodded. "Trotting the cobblestones?" "What's 'cobblestones'? No, I was on my scooter, and it broke. I fell." "Then, what? She guided you to this giant fountain with bright light flowing down from the top?" "No, silly. She just took me home. She had a fireplace – it was a little bit bright inside, but just a little. And then she kneeled and tied my shoelaces." It was Rada's turn to burst into tears. "Of course she did, David! You were never any good with your laces." They sat together for a while longer, in the dark. Then he lay down, and Rada told him his favourite story, about a little dinosaur who went out on a quest to find his baby brother; a story she'd made up, knowing his love of dinosaurs. He fell asleep, deeply, and they never talked about the dream again. The next day, Rada told David he would not have to go to church – any church, the Christian one or the synagogue – unless he wanted to. He didn't; he knew enough from his parents about each of their religions, and no one in the house was particularly preoccupied with that. Rada added he was free to make up his own faith as he felt it in his heart. And to welcome the dreams if they came back. "We're not strange people, David, for having such dreams," she said, "just a bit different – no better and no worse than others." Although Codrin apparently was never told, he went along with the plan without saying a word. Mysterious stuff to David … kind of like Santa.

Rada was an altogether different creature spiritually. David liked to imagine her like a baby dinosaur herself – part fierce and part cute; and certainly, an extinct species. Once, when he was a teenager, he heard her speaking on the phone with her mother. It was an intimate conversation; she was talking in a low voice: "It's never been a big deal for me, Mum. I turned out to be mystical but not religious – who knew this was a thing? It wasn't anyone's fault that I stopped going to the Cheder. You know how I am – how I have always been. Nobody could persuade me to do anything, least of all you guys. Sure, some of the kids – and their parents – stopped talking to me, but many didn't. And now we're all old and still live ten minutes from each other, and I say 'hi' to them and their families on the street. It wasn't nastiness as such – I was just kind of cast out. It made me stronger though, so, see? No big deal." She was lying, sparing the old woman's feelings. He knew that dreams were a big deal to her – because they were to him.

So, there it was, another remedy for David's ashen state of mind. Little by little, resurrected by his comeback home, the memories of his childhood dreams surfaced on top of the fresh and wounding ones from London. As the snow melted away completely and the streets tidied up, healing began in earnest. David could feel it at work, soothing and intimate but imperative like every mechanism programmed by life. For David, healing had started with an anonymous spark, the whisper in his dream, an impetus evading human probing. What followed, however, was tangible: the re-regulation of his daily rhythms and emotions. It could not be forced or rushed, but when it happened, it brought with it an ease and comfort that he lacked before. David could pinpoint the exact day and time his body finally relaxed in the familiar shape of the bed. He could tell when his psyche tuned back into the flow of life at home. No more pacing about the hallways in the middle of the night or searching the fridge for a late snack. No more impotent watching of others getting on with the daily business of life. Even if David did not like himself these days, he had retrieved the old knowledge that somehow, somebody out there still loved him.

Chapter 3. The Seesaw

"Do you know Benny Park? Of course you don't – it's tiny, right behind Avenue De Monkland. My mum used to take me there every day when I was little. Apparently, that's where I took my first steps. I still stop by sometimes when I come home from classes. They have a big seesaw right in the middle of the park; meet me there tomorrow." This was not his first date with Dina, but it was the one closest to her home. David was back to his habit of setting out the strategy: "I'm inching my way in, gaining territory."

He had met Dina at a recruitment fair organised by McGill University at their downtown campus. One of his chess friends, Freddie, who was majoring in Linguistics, had asked him to come along so he wouldn't feel too awkward networking on his own. David knew nothing about the world of editors or publishers: he had been a computer scientist for the past five years of his life. Still, he found himself following the panel discussion with some interest, as most of the big publishing houses were headquartered in London and their locations sounded familiar. "Did they just say Sloane Square? That's where my old office was," he remarked to Freddie, a tad louder than necessary. A curly-haired girl seated in front of them turned around and asked with wide eyes: "And you left it?" "Well, it's a long story," David suppressed a sigh, "… I doubt you're interested." Back in the hallway once the talks were over, while Freddie was touring the booths, the curly-haired girl walked up to him: "I *am* interested." Her eyes were sparkling behind a pair of large squarish glasses with bright-red frames – she was a bold one, observed David. He liked bold – he *needed* bold these days. His outgoing self was left back to … Sloane Square, of all places. Coming out of his shell and talking to people were now draining chores.

Dina was graduating in May with a Master's in History. She did not want to pursue research as a historian ("Too much injustice over the centuries to be uncovered") and did not fancy teaching either ("Too much brouhaha in the class"). She felt attracted to the quieter but more worldly field of publishing: "I could promote history books, or any books – think about it, the excitement of being the first pair of eyes, the first point of contact for an aspiring writer. Instant intimacy!" She had a naturally expressive face and was easily carried away. She probably knew it too, because she stopped, looking a bit embarrassed: "Too much too soon, eh? That's me, I'm afraid." "I'm not afraid – that's me, too. At least it used to be when I was your age," replied David wistfully. "And now you're what? A venerable thirty years old?" "Twenty-eight – but these few grey hairs were all acquired last year … in London, actually." He shared a few trite bits of information about the finance world and how it took a big hit in 2008. He did not feel like going into any depth for fear of boring his new acquaintance. But Dina, who knew little about the Recession other than what they'd been shown on the news in Canada, was keen to probe more: "Just because my family was not affected, it doesn't mean I should bury my head in the sand. I guess that's the historian in me speaking." Seeing how David hesitated, averting his eyes for a split second, she course-corrected for a second time: "If it's too raw for you, you know, this conversation can wait …" "No need to wait, really. I've seen a thing or two during my time in finance – stuff that needs to be heard by somebody – recorded even, I suppose. I'll tell you what: why don't you do your networking before they're winding down, and we can have a cup of coffee next week?"

They went on to meet every week, then twice a week, and finally every day. It was nothing short of a miracle: the miracle of David and Dina. By definition, a miracle eluded explanation. But if he had had to describe it, he would have said they were both easy-going and uncomplicated, yet they did not seem to lose their mystery to each other. For his part though, David knew perfectly well that he was holding something back: a feeling of being tainted and afraid. What if his past in London had damaged him in some deep, irreparable way? The doubt took root in his mind: what if it was this very woundedness that Dina found attractive? Had he met her fresh out of Yale, he might have been just another young graduate, naïve and slightly arrogant – and dull. By now, David had learnt to live with the "what if-s" of life. He knew he only had so much control about how he was perceived, even by Dina – especially by Dina, with her irrepressible spirit. But what he wanted – needed – to understand was why Dina had such a hold on *him*. What was her hidden wound? She always did her best to look happy-go-lucky, unscarred by the world around – why, then, did he feel so compelled to take care of her?

Dina was right; the seesaw in Benny Park was hard to miss. When he arrived, it was that undefined time of the day when nothing of importance happened – too late for toddlers to be out playing in the sand, too early for school kids to be invading the playground at lunch break. A couple of grandparents were sitting on a bench nearby, gently pushing a stroller back and forth while chatting quietly. David sat on the seesaw, pleased he'd found it free.

He lifted his gaze and caught a glimpse of the clouds above. It used to be his little secret as a schoolboy: for a few minutes every day, he would tune out the droning of his classmates and look up through the window to the clouds. He witnessed their daily ritual of passing through the sky, obstructing the sun for a minute or two, then following their tranquil paths. Inertial for the most part, the clouds would sometimes dissipate into the winds and then rejoin each other, playing out a heavenly drama in slow-motion, but never disturbed by any earthly business. Their spectacle never failed to give young David a sense of reassurance: as long as the clouds went on their predetermined trajectories, all was well with the world. "Funny how I haven't remembered this in twenty years," he pondered. "I should pick up my old habit again – only a child could come up with such a simple, wholesome one."

"You found it!" he heard Dina's rushed voice. She'd been running all the way from the bus stop. "Hi there! Have a seat, please," David invited her with a laugh. She couldn't, of course; he was keeping the other side of the seesaw high up. David rose and grabbed the seesaw to control its motion. "Please. And hold on to your book bag for added weight, otherwise you'll be way lighter than me." Now they were gently teetering, taking turns on their journey up, higher, infinitesimally closer to the clouds … and then back down again. "Hard day?" he asked. "Not really. I'm done with the final exams; now it's a straight line until the Defence." "Nice … and how's your thesis going?" "I've written most of it. I started with the Results, of course; the Intro can wait." "I hate intros – so many details; who needs them? Me, I prefer to get straight to the point." "I see … well, in that case … go for it," teased Dina. She was smiling down to him from her place up on the seesaw. It was noon time. As sunlight invaded the park, Dina's small silhouette picked up golden contours. David did not return her smile; in fact, Dina's sunny disposition was irritating him right now. He planted his feet firmly on the ground, pressing down, holding the seesaw for one minute too long. "Why are you keeping me at arm's length?" he asked morosely, then let go of his hold. "I am not!" protested Dina, coming down at some speed. "Why do you say that?" She sounded puzzled, but David was not about to relent. "For starters, you never tell me about your family, other than how your brother was annoying you when you were kids." "Well, there's not much to say." "Oh, yeah? How come I'm not allowed to meet any of them?" With a jerking move, David slammed his side of the seesaw into the ground. The impact made Dina jump a little in her seat, but she appeared mostly unfazed. After all, those were the laws of mechanical physics at play. "Of course you are allowed, David. I've just not found the right time yet." "I say today is as good a time as any. Right now, in fact – is it not why I'm here? We can go meet them now; they live, like, five minutes away." He had lifted Dina high up on the seesaw and was keeping her at a standstill – his small and shiny captive. "We might if you put me down," said Dina in a half-joking, subdued voice. "David … you are putting me down, right?" "They don't approve of me, do they? They know I'm nearly twenty-nine, back home and living with my parents … that I've been fired, perhaps? Just how much have you told them?" "Nothing! you asked me not to, and I didn't. And anyway, this is a subject that just never comes up." "You mean *I* … never come up. Why not? Your dear papa hasn't asked one question about his daughter's new boyfriend? Or maybe they don't even know that I exist … I'm not important enough to be mentioned – is that it?" "Put me down and I'll tell you." David went silent, stubbornly holding down the seesaw with his feet, his fists tight around the handle. He had the advantage of weight and he was going to use it. Then he looked up at Dina. Her hair was even curlier than usual, fluttering around her shoulders in the summery wind. Behind her, a cloud was making its undisturbed passage across the sky. She looked a bit like a fluffy cloud herself. The midday sun vanished behind the cloud for a second – an eclipse, that's what it was. And it was caused by him, with his moods and his awkwardness … and his shadow. The shadow side, that disavowed and vulnerable part in all of us. The part Clarissa had been so skilful in seeking and finding and punishing in David. The cloud passed by, dignified and elegant, leaving behind two funny creatures trapped on a seesaw. "Honestly, David, you're acting like a sulky child!" "I know. Promise you'll talk to me if I put you down? I mean, straight talk." Up on the seesaw, Dina was holding on to her seat with one hand, hugging her book bag with the other. She stood quiet for a few seconds, considering her options. "Ok – straight talk it is."

They sat down next to each other on the bench, which was now free. The two grandparents had left the scene, taking along the stroller and the baby. They must have found those two large children on the seesaw too weird, David surmised. "There was this guy before you …" started Dina. "Very nice guy, you know the Humanities type: articulate, mannered. Things were going well … we got far enough … and then he met my dad. And the thing was, David, that, for all the talk about open-mindedness and the Canadian liberal values and stuff … I never heard from him again. My dad said nothing … and we don't even look traditionally Muslim in our home – because we're not. But I was basically ghosted, without so much as a one-liner, a lame excuse. Now, I'm not saying what you think I'm saying … I've probably given him reasons, too. No, actually, that is exactly what I'm saying: that he was bigoted and left me in the dark. It hurt like nothing else had hurt before. For a long while, the world got deafeningly silent around me … you know the feeling?" David looked down – boy, did he know the feeling. "What was I to make of this, all on my own?" she asked in a pained voice. "That, when it comes down to it, when things get personal and people's futures are at stake – some men would rather run away than join a family like mine?"

There – he had exposed Dina's wound, turned her into a little girl with a big shadow – the same shadow of shame and betrayal that had been cast over him. Now he was feeling worse than ever. Dina was looking sideways at the empty seesaw, her hair covering her eyes, but David could feel her tearing up. Was this seesaw going to fade into a memory too, like the clouds … like London? A sketch with faded contours, a sign of what could have been. He clasped her hand and held it tight. "You're right; this world's a mess. But, Dina, for what it's worth, I am not going anywhere. Besides, your dad cannot be scarier than my mum. You've met her, twice in fact – she is the world's smallest, fiercest creature. I've seen big grown-up dudes intimidated by her presence; they shut up when she talks." "I didn't", observed Dina with a smile. "In fact, I thought I held my own quite well". "That is because you are braver than most."

***

That Dina had more job interviews than him came as no surprise to David. There was no job market for Quants in Montréal. There were big banks at every corner of the street but they were providing customer services only, with no product development or analysis teams behind the scenes. Toronto was closer to what he needed, but the Recession had hit it just as hard – and besides, hadn't he moved around enough? First Yale, then London; the time had finally come to be at home. The world might not have deemed this a courageous solution, but David did not care about the world right now. Yes, the adjustment was still painful, and so was any form of self-reflection. But once he realised how much he needed safety, connections – healthy ones, for a change – he knew that only home could give him that; it always did.

Giving up Finance, at least for the time being, was as effortless as it was logical. David's ego, just like his guilt, did not allow him to go back to Codrin about working as a chess coach. Instead, he took a part-time role as Data Analyst for the National Research Council – Rada had put him in contact with the team leader for Biology. Three days per week in Royalmount, writing a software package to predict protein structures, was all he could stomach these days. David had always felt comfortable around scientists, but now he liked them more than ever. He found them innocent, even amusing. Their benign gossip and jockeying for grants and publications seemed like a child's play compared to what he'd seen in banking. But, unlike finance, research was largely sheltered from the ruthlessness of the Recession. He knew it to be the case especially in Canada, where the government had research funding programmes in place across the provinces.

Meanwhile, Dina's summer was a string of one job interview after another – at least compared to David, who had an unusual amount of time on his hands. With her vivacity and enthusiasm, she made a good impression in the interviews. However, she was having a hard time securing an offer. Why? David had his own theory: she was too innocent, fresh out of university and unschooled about the so-called "real world". However, he chose to keep it to himself. After each interview, Dina had gotten into the habit of asking him to analyse the situation – what kind of people were involved, their roles, their verbal and non-verbal feedback, the likely outcome – all of it. "Because you are so good with people, David. *And* a good chess player – it must have something to do with that too. Your analysis is quicksilver, yet it goes deep." "Now you're just buttering me up!" David would answer, with a chuckle. Of course, it worked every single time. "What I do is trade off accuracy for the big picture. That's what it takes to make a fair prediction." "You don't trade anything, David. It's not a zero-sum game; it's your over-developed intuition." "My feminine intuition, perhaps? Say it, say it … it wouldn't be the first time I hear I'm a girly guy." "Well sir, you don't seem that girly to me," she would reply. And then, invariably, she would kiss him – and not a peck on the cheek. She was a great kisser; she liked to wrap her arms around him, bringing him closer each time, until they both knew they'd reached the limit of how close they could be outside the bedroom. And then they'd go inside the bedroom, still kissing – patient and generous with their moves at first, and then more driven and stubborn by the minute, swept up in glorious pursuit. He never had it so good, so triumphantly real – and never will. He had to grab this girl and keep her by his side, or else … He'd seen his world crumble before, and was not about to let it happen again. One time, as they were lying next to each other, in those moments when words are pointless and human reason is subdued by contentment, David took his chance: "You know, Dina, I could predict lots of things for you. Every day. And there are other ways to pay me for my services." "Oh? … I can't think of any better ways." "You could move in with me. As soon as you start earning, we can split the rent." "Split … the rent … oooh, that sounds sexy! I agree." "I am half serious." "I know, David … and I agree." She pulled him back, next to her warm skin, and gave him the ultimate proof of acceptance.

David and Dina were so busy with the move-in, they forgot to analyse her job interviews for a while. And, as soon as she stopped caring too much about the outcome, Dina sealed the deal.

Chapter 4. "Here's to Your Comeback!"

A workshop on Genomics was being held in Toronto in September, and David and a couple of colleagues were attending. His group at the NRC were looking to expand their research and needed someone to build a platform for gene analysis. This was David's opportunity to be more than an executant and take part in the scoping of the project – projects, to be more precise. It looked to be an entire portfolio, a solid, long-term investment, if he were to appraise it in financial terms. And he would have a word in its design.

It was here that he met Clive again after five years. He and Clive had been playing chess for Yale in the Universities League, with Clive as the junior, up-and-coming team member who shot straight to the top board in his first year. Clive was a mathematician, and David thought he looked the part: tall and wiry, with dreamy eyes, looking a bit lost in large crowds – a purist, at least compared to himself. What had this guy been up to all this time? A lot, as it turned out – he was now studying for his PhD at UoT, in Bioinformatics.

"Trust me, this is the way of the future," said Clive assuredly as he dug into his burger. The morning lectures were over and they were having lunch – a whole two-hour lunch break before the workshop sessions started. The place – Clive's favourite hangout – was unusually quiet for a student café. "Most people are not back to classes yet," he observed. "That's good," replied David, "we can actually hear each other. So, the way of the future, eh?" "Yep – and it's staring us in the face. It isn't Sci-Fi either: computers are quickly becoming more than a tool. If we build them at the right level of sophistication, before long they'll be able to predict anything for us." "That's perhaps true," David nodded, "I've seen how biologists are waking up to this idea. There is a lot of data to be mined by computers, now that the Genome project is completed." "That is exactly what I'm working on," jumped Clive, "I am ensuring the right level of sophistication. They needed a mathematician to do the modelling, and …" "And being a good one, and a good chess player, could not have hurt. I know you're right," acknowledged David with a peaceful smile, while being aware he fundamentally lacked his interlocutor's enthusiasm, "and it's not just Mathematics or Biology either. I remember watching 'A Beautiful Mind' – I had just finished high school back then, and was completely blown away. Around that time, game theory and its applications were all the rage ... That's what led me to do a minor in Economics, actually, and later on to work in Finance. Funny how I spent most of my time around computers, but my interest was piqued by one film – one human story. But when I walked outside the walled garden – the academia, research, lectures, and cozy venues like this one – the real world of economics was something else completely. You'll see after your PhD; it is a shock. And then the Credit Crunch hit … you were wise to ride it out." "By staying inside the walled garden," pointed Clive. "Precisely! I left it at a woefully wrong time, just before the Crisis, and joined the very field that got blamed for it. A field that will be scorned and scarred for decades to come." "See, that, to me, is flawed thinking. This backlash on the finance sector smells of slave morality." Noticing David's puzzled look, Clive decided to elaborate a bit: "You know, a philosophy that is emotionally rewarding for the masses and the mediocre, but singles out the bold and competent, making them look blameworthy in some ways. I take it you haven't read Nietzsche? The likes of him, of Ayn Rand, or Sartre – the great iconoclasts, the rebels and the cynics?" "No, and I'm afraid I have no attraction for any of these concepts. I remember enjoying Camus in school, though – the whole idea that we can squeeze out meaning from a universe that's fundamentally indifferent to us. My mind works more along these lines. See, I'm no iconoclast – no visionary, either. I am one of those irreparably wholesome people – which makes for dull company, I guess." "Nonsense!" Clive cut him short again, and carried on with gusto: "You are who you are! I remember our time at Yale: you stood out from day one. Where did that go, by the way – your chutzpah?" "Drowned in the Thames, I suppose. I'm kidding; I grew up. Besides, I wasn't all that special. I just didn't like to outsource my thinking." "Like I am doing with my philosophers?" "Maybe ... though in small doses, these guys are helpful. I'd stay away from self-professed gurus, though – nobody has unbound access to wisdom. We all need some form of guidance, at least in times of crisis. Of course, I wouldn't wish you to understand this experientially, like I had to. That would take care of your chutzpah, all right. Who was this?" asked David, as Clive greeted an athletic-looking woman sporting a wide smile. "Speaking of chutzpah ... this was Vicky, our student union president. We are good friends." "But you guys don't see eye to eye politically? I don't suppose she is the type to take kindly to slaves and masters and all that verbiage." "Hey, watch how you talk about the Greats, man! It is a metaphor and a matter of debate. She is a lot like the old you – driven, going places, and very open-minded. Would you like to come to one of our meetings some time? They can be fun, you know." Clearly, there was a lot more to Clive than met the eye. "Some time, yeah ... but tell me something else, please: am I going to hear about you in ten years' time? You know, in a big way? Like in 'Clive, Canada's new Prime Minister' way?" "Ha! As if you guys are ever going to accept an American at the helm! But you are on to something: Canada is a country after my own heart, and I have already applied for residency. Give me twenty years ..." "Nah, in twenty years we'll all be washed-up ... just look at our parents." "I wouldn't be so sure, David. Not if technology has anything to say about that." "Technology ... and Providence." It was Clive's turn to stare at him with wide, inquiring eyes. David chose not to explain himself; it was too early in the day for this conversation. "Anyways, let me finish my rant about the real world," he proceeded. "Thanks to our beautiful minds, we now have game theory to predict the best move at all times. Which, in principle, should make everyone a winner. And here is the point where the machines will soon become smarter than us. The slaves will be the masters, if you will. Why? Because they're being programmed to have a sound psychology – by people like you and me, let's say. We engineer them with level heads and one clear goal: to optimise outcomes for everybody. But, in our heart of hearts, is this what we humans want? Has our psychology evolved in parallel with our skills? We're still at the level of Genghis Khan when it comes to winning or losing: we cannot see ourselves as winners unless the guy next to us is a loser." "So, what are you saying?" "I'm saying, be prepared to deal with this when you exit your academic bubble." "I don't know that I'll ever exit! And, David, I don't plan to; I wouldn't last a day! I may be nerdy and idealistic, but I protect myself ...

I can see better ways to use my mental energy than dealing with the randomness of the real world, as you call it." Clive looked him straight in the eyes, earnestly, as if waiting for his approval. "Seriously, man. This is where I belong – in research, surrounded by ideas and talking heads. For now, we are still using computers as tools. But they can also learn … and they will. There is this new thing I hope to work on over the coming years: machine learning." "It's not that new," retorted David, "I took a course on neural networks as a student, and yes, it sounded spicy. But how far can you get by recognising people's handwriting from a bunch of pictures?" "That's what they are able to do now, but give them twenty years and they'll be recognising illnesses from a bunch of scans. I told you: this isn't Sci-Fi anymore." "In that case, you, my friend, might be twenty years ahead of the game," smiled David, downing his mineral water. Lunch was over and he wanted to say something nice to Clive before they parted. After all, it was obvious the guy was still looking up to him after all these years. Why did intelligent people appreciate him while the stupid ones felt free to mock him – or worse, manhandle him? "You're in a good place, Clive – using your brain, meeting interesting people. Hey, you used to do it over the chessboard … now you can take over the world!" "Laugh all you want," replied Clive, visibly flattered, "we'll speak in twenty years." David went quiet, as he sometimes did with his dad too. These were the moments he tacitly admitted the person in front of him might have been smarter than him, or more lucid, or both. Clive sure did not like silence today; he launched on a last-minute elevator pitch: "You could come over, you know, join my research team. You have a solid footing in Bioinformatics already, and they would love someone with industry experience … someone who's learnt the gold standard of programming rather than the patchwork we do here. You know the chess team at UoT is the best in the Leagues?" "Is it now? Hmm … thanks, Clive. It's nice to know I still have options. For now, I think I'll stay in Montréal. I've got a good thing going on there …" "Ok … I see … and does she have a name?"

***

Dina's first job, as an Account Executive in a publishing house in Laval, was going remarkably well. The commute was reasonable and David was giving her a ride twice a week, on the days he didn't work. On passing her probation, she was immediately promoted to Senior Account Executive. This raised her spirits and her confidence; she offered to take on more projects and was now building her own, albeit small, customer base. This meant putting in longer hours, so David was called to pick her up later and later every week. Winter was coming and, with it, the dreaded early evenings. Ever since his episode with Clarissa, David had taken a dislike to dark roads and ambiguous trips home.

One afternoon, as he was driving her back from Laval on a pitch-black highway, Dina casually asked him: "How would you like to go back to London?" "What do you mean – now? As in, a holiday?" "No, not a holiday. They want to send me to their London office next year. My publishing house." "To work there?" "No, David, to check out their new and amazing shopping mall, Westfield I think it's called ... you know, the one that has defied the credit crunch? So, what do you say – should we?" David did not like Dina's smarty-pants tone. For the rest of the ride, he did not speak a word; he focused on the traffic instead. If they hit a bottleneck on the A-40, they could be stuck for hours. Dina seemed to understand his silence. She did not pressure him while on the road but, as soon as they entered their apartment building, she looked up to him and held his gaze for a while, candidly, as if to say: *"Just tell me something. You know I'd never hurt you."* David knew she deserved better than the silent treatment. "Fundamentally, Dina … I don't want to go. If this were all happening a year ago, maybe, I'm not sure. But now … with so much water under the bridge, as the Brits say …" "I understand: they were assholes to you; they kicked you out. But it doesn't have to be the same this time around." "You're right, in principle … there's something else though. It wasn't even that I got kicked out, it was the way they went about it. It was perverse and callous." "But you are with me now!" "Yeah, Dina, and you know what we'll look like? Like the deaf leading the blind … some couple!" "Since when do you care about how we look like? And are we really that naïve, unfit and unsophisticated? Is that how you see us – how you've seen us all along? Explain to me, please." They got inside the apartment and David switched on the lamp in the living room. It was a spacious room – at least once they'd removed the second, unnecessary couch, not after much deliberation with the landlord. The look and feel of the apartment were cozy and warm – Dina's work – and the gadgets were up-to-date and cool – David's. How could she leave this all behind in a blink? What did she think she'd find elsewhere? And why London of all places? "That is the wrong question to ask, Dina. And, just by asking it, you really do look naïve and unsophisticated. The problem is not us; it's them … the corporate culture … or Britain, or both … the way they view people as objects. I've been hanging out with the Ivy League boys and girls for four years … and yes, some were arrogant and entitled, and thought they were the centre of the world and maybe saw themselves as future Nobel Prize winners and whatnot … but they were fundamentally whole. Sound. They made sense. Some of the things I've seen in my last workplace were … broken, dangerous." "Things? You mean, people …?" "I mean broken people doing dangerous things. But see, interestingly, these people were never a danger to themselves. That's why I never bought the 'madness' argument. When people are capable of keeping their nerve in front of others but they do nasty, abusive things to you one-to-one, when nobody's watching, that is not madness … it is a fundamental lack of backbone." "Well, that was then … and it happened to you. Of course, it wouldn't hurt me if you gave me details about these 'broken people' … but I get it. I won't prod. What I can tell you for a fact though, is that it won't happen to me." "Let us stop here, Dina, please. Every word coming out of your mouth is proof that I am right. And, on this occasion, I really hate to be right."

They lay the dinner table together, in silence, each following their own side of the argument in their mind. David had brought takeaways from his favourite Middle Eastern place in the neighbourhood. Dina usually loved to criticise Middle Eastern food for being nothing like the real thing, but not this time. They quietly devoured it. Then, Dina got out a bottle of champagne. He had not seen the bottle before – she must have purchased it during lunch break, as soon as she'd been made the offer. David realised with bitterness how happy she actually felt, and how big a moment this was for her. She filled two coffee mugs – they did not have any champagne glasses at home

– and offered one to David. "Here's to your comeback!" Her smile was more effervescent than the bubbles. He knew Dina too well to mistake the champagne for a peace offering. They barely finished sipping the last bubbles, when she resumed the argument from the exact place she had left it: "You are not right this time, David. You don't have many blind spots, but this is one of them, believe me. I am not going to have the same problems as you – simple as that. Look at me now: I'm working with lots of different people and I am doing great; and, believe me, Canadians are no saints either. And if you're going to say that my world is less about money and more about books, you need to stop right there. There's not one idealistic soul in my office. Sure, they read and commission books, and sometimes fall in love with those books, but what do you think these people do in their spare time? They talk about their latest date, TV show, purchase, whatever … they gossip about others, about who got promoted and why … and that's all fine by me. And you know why? Because I'm more like them – more mediocre. No, no …" she continued, talking over him, "Please don't protest; it's true … starting with my looks. Plus, I think I've got some basic training through all my years of dealing with my mum. And that's the other thing, David: your folks love you too much – that's kind of a sin when you're a parent, you know? Your child grows up lacking immunity to people's meanness. Whatever the reason, Freudian or not, I am perceived as less threatening by the others. And I intend to use this fully to my advantage. Our advantage. Dina and David, the Canucks, are going to show them how it's done."

Dina was beyond determined; she was childishly stubborn. Well, maybe "childish" was not the word. If he was being fair, she had every right to be insistent – going to London had been her dream for as long as she could remember, her great chance to get out in the world. Who was he to deny her that? He put a stop to the discussion but asked her for a few days to mull over the possible scenarios, pretending he was weighing on important matters. Eventually, of course, he gave his nod. In doing that, the next move became painfully clear: he had to find a job in London.

***

Whom could he talk to of those colleagues that had stayed behind? David had left London in such a turmoil; there was no time to say good-bye or ask for people's contact details. He'd had a group of friends and beer buddies, four guys who met on Fridays after work. They used to compare notes and inside stories – company gossip of low calibre. A most unserious bunch … except for Raoul, the oldest. Raoul always left their gatherings a couple of hours early: he had a son – a toddler – and did not want to miss his bath time. When Raoul did gossip, it was for a good reason, and always with a grain of factual information. Whatever was he up to now – and how had he survived? He might have gone back home; both he and his wife were from Mauritius. But then again, he might not have. David had saved no email addresses, but there was the odd chance they'd texted one another at some point. He searched his phone and there it was, one message from Raoul, exactly a year ago. "I could just call him back – but how to justify the silence? For sure, the whole bunch was let go soon after me. We've all been silent, which is normal. Which guy is keen to get in touch and share his sorrows? By comparison with them, especially Raoul, I've probably had it easy – I'll need to bear this in mind when I call."

David's worries dissipated when he heard Raoul on the phone. He greeted David with his usual calm voice, which sounded pleasantly surprised. "Hey, David! It's been ages. We're doing ok – thanks for asking. You know I've never heard from any of the other guys? But they're all here in London. You were the only one who left the country – and what a mess they've made of your departure! I should have called, but …" "Better you didn't. Thing is, Raoul, in the first month or so, I was completely out of sorts … I couldn't even talk to my folks properly. I just wanted to hide!" "Here, we hit rock bottom around May. My severance package was gone – we'd used it to pay the nursery fees, which are obscene in London, as you know … oh, actually, you don't know. So, I was firing like ten applications daily, not getting any answers; I got the feeling some of the job postings were fake, just put out there to show activity. And then in June, we pulled our son out of the kindergarten. We had to, and we came up with some lame explanations: 'Honey, Daddy would like to spend more time at home. You'll get to play lots more with him … yaay! … when he's not waiting by the phone, that is.' Poor kid, I'll never forget the look on his face. They're not totally clueless, you know? But still, he was only three years old. A part of him was happy to just have me around all the time, stressed out as I was. And actually, we became best friends. Our supreme treat was to watch 'Cars', the movie, together – twice a day, every day. And then we'd practise racing his toy cars in the park. At least last Spring was nice in London; we were not stuck indoors. But otherwise, we were stuck in every imaginable way." "I am not sure I can imagine, honestly. Did you not think of leaving? For me, another reason I went back to Canada was my work visa." "Oh, yeah. Well, as you know, for those like us who are not British, the visa clock never stops ticking – it doesn't care about the world collapsing. We stayed – we really needed to get that British residency. I mean, we'd already been in Britain for five years at that point. We had to keep clocking the time, so we scrambled by from one month to another. My wife took up a job in a care home. We only saw her briefly in the evenings, but that was a lucky break for us – it certainly helped pay the rent. And, as a family, we managed to survive on less, much less, than what people like us used to earn." "Same here – when I came back to Montréal, I took a salary cut with my eyes closed. They did not even ask how much I made before – nobody cared." "It's like a parallel universe out there. I knew that from my time as a researcher, so I was not in shock like the others. I re-adapted – all three of us did. Do you not think we had been spoiled working in Finance? Maybe some people were right in saying the bubble had to burst. They're holding us responsible; that's for sure." "I don't agree – we did work hard. And studied hard. You, for example, you have a PhD, right? from the London School of Economics – that's not for everyone." "You want to know the funny part? The smartest thing I did when I was earning well was not to gamble with my income in the stock market. I thought about my son and saved money in the most unsophisticated ways. Which goes exactly against the grain of all my research at the LSE. And you know why I acted like this? Because, at heart, we're immigrants. Growing up, I've never seen any investor in my family or our circle of friends. What do you make of that?" "I think you guys were smart and your psychology was solid. People study Psychology for all the wrong reasons and in all the wrong settings. They ask us to look inside to the degree where we weaponize our ability for self-reflection and turn it against ourselves. No wonder our capacity for action is annihilated. That's not what those in power are doing though – they look towards the outer world, at causes and effects, and act. It would behoove psychologists, I think, to embed their theories in a systems context – like economics for example. The psychology of financial decisions – now that's something I'd like to see studied. I also think the blame that's piled on us at the moment is excessive, and so do friends of mine. How is that fair for a guy like you to be stuck at home, jobless … for what, a year? When did you actually find a job?" "Only a couple of months ago – with a hedge fund. They call me a 'special associate' and I do pretty much anything they ask. My wife has kept her job too, part time – we cannot risk going through this again, being completely exposed financially. These days, we're trying to restore our rainy-day savings. And we've restarted kindergarten, also part time. The little guy still comes to me at weekends to watch 'Cars' together. He knows every single reply by heart, every character, and he enacts each one with just the right tone and mimic. He's bound to become Britain's next Laurence Olivier – all due to the Recession. I guess we have to be grateful for our misfortunes, and all that sort of crap." "Gosh, I never stopped to think how hard it must have been to put a family through this." "Worst part was faking it. Not to my wife – she's dealt with it magnificently – but to my parents in Mauritius. They'd phone to ask for updates every single week, compulsively. I guess their anxiety was getting the better of them. In the beginning, I would tell the truth – that I was still waiting for an answer. And you know what they'd do? They'd turn it around like I wasn't trying hard enough. Like there was some job out there, just waiting for me to grab it, and I was saying no." "They never fully understand, do they? They think we're brilliant geniuses or something, and that the world should stop and pay attention to us." "So, what I ended up doing, was fake it. That was the real nightmare. You should have heard me: 'We're doing fine, mum. I have some applications on the roll … I'm getting pretty close. There is this guy who's putting me in touch with another guy, and we are talking next week. So, there's no need for you to call again. Unless you guys have any hints or leads, if you believe there's anything for me back home. That would be good to know – soon.' And, like my son, they bought it. They bought my act because they love me." "Yeah, well, sometimes a parent's love is suffocating. And certainly not very effective in a crisis." "I used to think the same when I was younger. But you know what? I stopped when I became a dad. You'll see one day …" David could not bring himself to ask Raoul if he had any leads or contacts in his new workplace that could be of help. The answer was clear as daylight. Why make the poor man come up with one more lie?

Chapter 5. Desert Calls

The awkward and inevitable moment of "meeting the family" had come at last. Dina and David were keen to simply tick the box and move on. It did not have to be a great success, just not a complete disaster, they reassured each other. Their parents seemed to take it much more seriously though: after all, they had been made to wait for half a year. As the evening started, four middle-aged people were fumbling for words – especially Rada, who was seated next to Dina's mum. David knew his mother had a hard time relating to other women; in fact, Rada could count all her friends on one hand, and more than half were men. After about an hour, she and Anne had exhausted the usual topics. They'd started with grandchildren: Anne had two, from her son, and was an involved grandmother; Rada had none and listened wistfully to the baby stories. After about half an hour, they'd moved to places to go and things to do. Anne did not share Rada's fondness for the Botanical Gardens and open spaces in general, but was an expert in interior design – another black box to Rada, for whom her old, round samovar table was the epitome of style. Finally, the conversation landed on the Québecois politics. Here, Rada came to life a little, as there was always something to be said about the government's latest "gaffe", and she was not the type to hold back a political opinion. "I must have come across as intense and shy at the same time," she lamented to David afterwards. "Well, that's exactly how you *are* – but in small doses, luckily." Making light of his mum's social persona was always working as intended. David knew just how to give Rada the kind of reassurance she needed: that, for all her quirky, intimidating vibe, and for all her past as an outcast of sorts, she was a good-natured woman with no agenda to push on others, and those who met her sensed that.

Dina appeared less preoccupied with her mum; Anne was worldly and could easily get along with anyone. In the carefully allocated space of a single afternoon, Anne's inner distance, which had been a source of pain for Dina over the years, remained well hidden underneath her bubbly demeanour. The parent she worried about was her dad, as she'd told David since their early days in Benny Park. David's first impression of Mehdi was quick and clear: "Here is a man who feels a duty to be hospitable – it must be in his DNA. He cares little if we are boring or entertaining – he simply does not evaluate people in these terms. We are his guests; period." That was the surface though; like his wife, Mehdi had layers. David knew from Dina that her father's moods were not exactly a recipe for social success. Mehdi could easily slip into a sullen silence when not feeling at ease. Other times, he would become verbose and prone to philosophising in a pessimistic, bitter sort of way. If the invisible fence around her mum was palpable to Dina, with Mehdi, she had full access – but had to walk on eggshells. To David, Dina's father seemed a bit like his mum – two strange people without a social filter, but who meant well – too well for their own good, perhaps.

A wintry sun was setting over the apartment in Notre-Dame-de-Grâce. David and Dina were watching it together from the balcony, huddled under David's coat. Underneath them, on Avenue de Monkland, the pedestrians were coming in and out of the stores, lining up at the bus station, getting their last bank transactions done before heading back home. It was the peaceful white noise of ordinary life – a peace taken for granted, a peace they were blissfully unaware of. "So – what do you think about him?" David knew how much she cared about his answer. Time to use the light touch: "Your papa sure doesn't come with a user's manual!" "I know," sighed Dina, prepared to hear more. "But look, that's why you like me – I am an open book." "You are a darling!" Relieved, Dina glanced back towards the living room and saw the two women contemplating the carpet while the men were bringing out dinner plates from the kitchen. "We're going to need an intervention," she whispered to David, "or they'll all die of boredom".

Nobody expected Codrin to step in and rescue the evening – not even himself. There was no alcohol, and he was longing for his usual glass of red wine in the evenings, which served to make him voluble and bring out the dad jokes. "And here is the chorba," announced Mehdi, pouring the hot soup, which filled the air with fragrances of mint and coriander. It was an instant hit. "Oh, but you've surpassed yourself, my friend!" Anne exclaimed, to general approval. Codrin was astonished: "I can't believe you call it 'chorba'! That's exactly how we call it in Romania – only we make ours with dill and parsley. It's just as tasty – well, what do I know, I haven't tasted it in years!" he added ruefully. Then quickly, so as not to touch a nerve with his wife: "Rada is not really into soups." "Yeah, I'm more of a meat and potatoes kind of girl," she quipped, hoping – and managing – to get a smile out of the young ones. "The secret is, you have to serve it hot," explained Mehdi. "But not too hot or we'll burn ourselves," added Codrin. "Then we'll have to blow into the yoghurt," he continued wryly. "And I was afraid we wouldn't have any dad jokes tonight!" teased David. Now it was Mehdi's turn to be surprised: "Wait – you have the same proverb in Romanian? He who gets burned on hot chorba blows into the yoghurt?" "Absolutely; I had no idea it's Arabic too," replied Codrin. "You just love to make your jokes literal, Dad." "Well, that's my form of wisdom, David – take it or leave it."

As he was helping himself to another serving, Codrin noted matter-of-factly: "I'm getting fat – too fat for a baseball coach. I have seen some fat coaches in my time, but never in baseball." "How come you're coaching baseball, anyway?" asked Dina. "Oh, it's a long story. I tried to make it in baseball back in Romania, but you can imagine my success. It wasn't that they only cared about football; handball was popular too. Not to mention volleyball, which got very far in the '60s: at some point, the European final was played between two Romanian teams. But traditionally, we've always had the 'oina', a sort of poor man's baseball. That was my thing. I wasn't just good at it; I was obsessed. Like any young man, I needed an outlet for my energy. And I wanted to spread the word about it … form a team – one of international standards – and go to tournaments and show the world our greatness." "Codrin is a bit quixotic that way," mused Rada, "once he's hooked, he's hooked. He'll never retire from coaching." "A-ha, so that's where David is getting his ambition from!" pointed Anne. "I'd rather call it 'passion'. And yes, it certainly is not from me," observed Rada with a smile. She was the slowest of the group, the only one still working on her soup. But she was finally feeling chatty: "They dragged me into the girls' football team once and I ran away at half break. I was small and uncompetitive, and the sight of those leggy girls, fast and muscular and bumping into me, filled me with fear. I never went back on the field again." In his good-natured way, David was poised not to let his mother off the hook:

"You have had your ambitions, though, and most of them involved me … with dubious results." A smattering of laughter rose round the table. "But how did you end up in Canada?" Now she had found Codrin's subject of interest, Dina was determined to go on. "Oh, I was so annoyingly persistent, the Sports Federation allowed me to attend an international baseball game – to learn the ropes, as it were. By then, of course, I knew a thing or two about the sports scene in Romania – across all Eastern Europe, really. We had imported the Soviet model, and sports were revered by the Soviets, as you know – but only the vetted sports! A buddy of mine, fellow at the Sports Academy, was trying similar things in karate; it didn't pick up much at the time but he fared better nonetheless. I was the black sheep of my class, with my interest in a 'capitalist' sport. Anyway – they couldn't send me to America, of course, but they said yes to Canada, which had become popular after the big Expo in '67. The Federation had some funding in the run-up to the Olympic Games, and Montréal was on everyone's lips. So, they sent me … and I did not return. It sounds selfish, saying it loud like that, but I could not see any future for myself. Trying to teach baseball in Romania was like … like teaching swimming in the Sahara".

"Swimming in the Sahara … I'll say!" Mehdi interjected with a light in his eyes. "That's where I'm coming from, you know. We left Algeria during the Independence War; I was a small boy back then. We were among the lucky ones … our relatives, the friends we left behind … some didn't make it … and we could not find out what happened. The little that we did see on TV was nothing short of heart-wrenching. And then, of course, the Black Decade, which people talked about even less. Years and years shrouded in deadly silence." With a shudder, Mehdi stopped in his tracks, as if he forbade himself from reviving those images. He sighed deeply and clasped his hands, staring into the ground. David now understood his sombre moods were not without a reason. But, where other guests used to avert their eyes, these ones held space. In the stillness that fell over the dining room with the last glint of sunset, there was a sense of togetherness, subdued but deep. The older and the younger sat quietly, breathing the tranquil air around them. Unlike the passers-by on Montréal's boulevards, this group was fully present. And supper was over.

In a soft voice, Codrin broke the silence: "When I left Romania in '75, I was completely on my own; I couldn't allow myself to put anyone in danger. With every year, it was getting harder to breathe. Ten years before, the Communists had put their rising star in power … a young guy from the countryside, kind of dumb-looking but well liked inside the party. A poster boy, is how these kids would call him. Nobody knew then he would become so dangerous. Another decade of tyranny, that's what I've managed to avoid … Did you ever go back?" he asked, turning towards Mehdi. "We took the children to Sétif a couple of times in the 2000s, before they started university. I am not sure what they made of it, but, thank God, they saw it in peace. The place seemed recovered, at least on the outside. The people? No one can tell." "It was really a beautiful place, Papa," Dina reassured him, "mysterious but modern… and surprisingly green. I'd like to show it to David some day." Mehdi carried on in a pensive tone: "I was so busy when the kids were young, always in the hospital, taking emergency calls at all hours … I never had the time to think about my past. I'm still busy these days, but my thoughts drift away … and home is on my mind more and more. Even the desert, which I remember visiting with my parents a long, long time ago. I feared I had forgotten all about it, but these days, I close my eyes and I just see it. It's the middle of winter in Canada and I can feel the burning air on my skin." "Me, I've never looked back," Codrin shrugged, "and I'm not sure I ever will." "Whatever would be left for you there anyway?" Rada's reply came almost automatically. It sounded like a topic they had discussed many times, and Rada had a ready-made argument for the occasion. "You wouldn't recognise the place, Codrin; you wouldn't know how to start talking to people." "That's how *I* feel sometimes," Mehdi jumped in. We must be getting old. Going back now, for us ..." he followed, heading to the balcony to light up a cigarette, "... would be ..." "Like swimming in the Sahara," concluded Codrin.

***

The last thing David needed at the start of 2010 was a New Year's resolution. Well, he had been handed one, whether he liked it or not. Applying for jobs in London – the second time around – was a loathsome affair. There was the psychic baggage from his first stint in London, still unclaimed, weighing him down. And yet, a part of him was waiting to get back into the game. But now in 2010, after two embattled years in the capital markets, things set in motion with the inertia of a truck. Response rates to his applications were low – very low. By March, David had completed a handful of programming tests, never to hear from those companies again. Luckily, this was not his first rodeo in the world of hedge funds and banks. He knew that programming tests – which he had always passed with flying colours, courtesy of the merciless assignments and exams at Yale – were more of a "go away, leave us alone" tactic by the employers. After a few more weeks, he managed to secure his first and only interview, for an Actuarial Analyst role. It involved the joyous work of analysing people's risk of dying to set their life insurances at the right level. But Actuaries were on more solid ground than Quants these days, so David tried his best to sound keen over the phone. Then, silence. He followed up by email and received a polite rejection. At least he wasn't ghosted: they'd found somebody with prior experience in life insurance products, which was fair enough.

After a while, David had come to expect the poorest outcomes. He was not being defeatist – he was being real, he told himself. He almost felt comfort at the thought that London might not be on the cards after all. None of this job search drama was shared with Rada or Codrin – what was the point, when they were so happy to have him around? "This is what being lucky looks like. *It looks like me, now*. We're still deep in Recession and I have the luxury of waiting. I am not panic-stricken, nor trapped. I've got a place to live, work to do, people to talk to. My small student loan – thanks, Québec scholarship system! – is almost paid, without robbing my folks in the process. Most of my colleagues back in London have spent all of last year doing exactly what I am doing now – over and over, with loans to pay and no alternatives and no way out. Looking for work in a market that was irreversibly broken, keeping afloat on a career path vilified by the entire world. Riding the daily rollercoaster of applications, inquiries, rejections – all this under the pressure of everyday survival. Finding "creative" ways to pay the rent – side gigs or house shares. And, worst of all, being alone. No money to go out with friends or on a date. A random phone call, one per week: the sales people. I hope I'll never find out just how bad things can get … I'm not as brave as others, nor do I need to be. I'm lucky."

He was having lunch at the NRC canteen one day, when his mobile phone rang. He rarely dined alone, but this time the rest of the group were off to a research conference in Vancouver. It was a British number; he picked up. "Hello, I am Diane. I'm following up to your call with Mike, the recruitment agent. It went very well, and your test afterwards was flawless." David could not remember which agent they were talking about – he'd been in touch with at least a dozen over the past few months. "We'd like to have a second interview with you, David – ideally, we'd fly you in, though phone is fine for the moment." "Why, thank you! Are you the Cambridge group?" "No, we are based in London – in Chelsea, actually. We are a relatively small group but we are growing. Fantastic location, new office. We might be opening another one in New York if things go well. We offer a gym membership too – all our Quants enjoy it." "So, this is for a Quant role – not IT?" "Well, David, with your background and experience, IT would be a bit of a waste of time, don't you think? Not to speak 20 k less in salary. We're talking Sterling, of course." David blinked. Who were these people and why were they being nice to him? "Right, sure, I mean … Quant is what I had in mind all along, but of course, since last year's developments …" "That is precisely what we wanted to explore in our interview. You see, we did not suffer so badly from the Crash. We only had one main client at the time, who managed to survive … As a matter of fact, against all odds, we thrived. I believe our secret has been diversity. We have attracted a small but loyal pool of international talent. Our Quants are wonderful – we have an cxcellent Senior Quant and are looking to hire a junior one soon."

"Well, I'm not exactly junior anymore." "Precisely – we feel you would do great as the Quant team leader. There is a salary scale, of course, commensurate with experience. So, you would start a bit lower on this scale – mind you, that's still £10 k above the senior level. It is a leadership position; you'd be reporting directly to the Head of Strategy." "That sounds … like a fantastic opportunity, Diane! We definitely should proceed with the second interview. Can I just ask, what exactly about my application has stood out for you?" "Your CV is impressive – I'm sure I'm not the first to tell you that. Your academic excellence, your experience. But also, there is someone here in the team who knows you well. She spoke very highly of you." "She …?" "Ms Clarissa Warpley. You worked together last year for one of our competitors. They fared much worse than us in the current climate, I'm afraid. Surely, you do remember her?"

For a few seconds, the canteen turned shaky and blurry around David; it was as if he needed a pair of glasses to refocus the entire universe. He grabbed the edge of the table and put the phone down. Why was he being followed by Clarissa's ghost? And how incestuous was their industry anyway? "Hello … David …? Are you still there?" He steadied himself: "Yeah, I believe we've lost connection for a second … of course … Clarissa Warpley. That's very kind of her. I am available for an interview in April. I'll need to take time off from my current role, check with my manager." "No problem, we can wait a little. I see you're based in Montréal now – would relocation be a problem?" "No, not at all." David was lying. He knew that Dina was so keen, but needed – and wanted – to check with his team leader whether his contract at NRC could be extended, and under what circumstances. He owed that to this group; one did not leave a perfectly decent job at the drop of a hat. He was lying because he was on autopilot – the deferential, "let's get along and not make a fuss" state of mind, which earlier, when he was of Clive's age, he used to call "cowardice". His dizziness had not fully gone away. Maybe he *was* in need of real glasses – rose-coloured ones, to filter out the irony of his reality. "Would I be working with Clarissa?" He needed clarity from Diane on this one thing from the get-go. "Not directly; she's in a different team." "That's absolutely fine! Well, I would love to find out more about the role," David added, trying to end the conversation on a high note, "it would be good to make a comeback in this way."

After years in London, David had come to know the British people quite well. At least well enough to tell the second interview was going to be a formality and he was going to ace it no matter what he said. He had been endorsed by one of them – that was enough in their eyes. Although, for all the trash-talking he indulged in when it came to the Brits, he could not deny he was becoming one of them. A non-confrontational people-pleaser who said one thing and thought and felt another. His great excuse? He was doing it all for Dina. "But what if my reasoning is all BS? What if I still have a thing for little Miss Warpley? Well, that would label me forever as a masochist. Am I a masochist? Nah … it is for Dina ... she is practically forcing me. I am not masochistic, but I sure am feeling disproportionately guilty saying 'no' to a woman. Also, I need to be fair here and give Clarissa the benefit of the doubt. If she's put in a good word, it means she's genuinely sorry. And if she is so contrite, she is bound to behave better this time around or at least stay away from me. No one can do such a horrific thing twice

– she cannot be so unaware of herself. Unless she has a broken mental record, repeating some childhood dynamics she is trapped in, and which has nothing to do with me. That *would* be dangerous. Ok; I'll go, but it won't mean I let Clarissa off the hook – especially if she starts acting out her weird stuff again. And first things first, I have to talk to Dr. Peng." Dr. Peng was the Biology team leader at the NRC, an exceedingly affable and diplomatic man. Thinking of him, David's inner discourse took on encouraging tones: "See? Dr. Peng is good at pulling off this little strategy – he never rocks the boat but keeps a constant eye on politics and funding. So maybe what I think is pathetic about me – my dislike of confrontation – would be called 'tactful' in other circles. Like, for example, in a managerial position – which is where I could be in London." His meetings with Dr. Peng were always casual, held around a cup of coffee at the canteen. They set one up as soon as the team got back from Vancouver. David was surprised by Dr. Peng's reaction to his potential job offer: he congratulated him. It felt a little disappointing: weren't they going to try to keep him? Was he really so replaceable within the group? He risked a moment of honesty: "That said, Dr. Peng, I do not really have to go, not even for the interview. I love my work here and I'd like to think I'm good at it." "You are good, David; we're all extremely pleased with you. In fact, the Materials group leader was asking if they could perhaps share you." "Sorry, what do you mean exactly?" "You see, David, unfortunately, high-skilled programmers and data analysts are considered a different kind of resource here. We are a bunch of scientists, chasing the latest research trends, but not always willing to learn the technical ropes, so to speak. Not many people understand the value of a dedicated expert like you. So, when it comes to computational projects, we operate through fixed-term contracts. Your contract is up for renewal after the first 6 months. Then we might ask you to work for the Materials Science group … and then in 6 months' time, we'll reassess again." Of course – what was he thinking? Never mind that Dr. Peng's position at NRC was permanent and secure, David reflected with a twinge of bitterness; others around him had to fight for their own jobs twice a year, every year. The older man took note of his reaction and patted him on the back: "That's why I say to you: Congratulations! A permanent job is a fantastic accomplishment, especially in this climate. If it pans out, you shouldn't take it for granted."

So, whether he wanted or not, London was back on the cards for 2010. David knew his parents would not like the news and was still feeling guilty about snapping at Codrin in his first months back home. Yet somehow, over the coming days, they understood. As always with those two, there was no big discussion, no family drama. But he could feel nostalgia taking a seat around the samovar table as the new tea time guest to an ageing couple. One weekend, as he and Dina were paying them a visit, David finally felt ready to say something. Just then, Codrin blurted with a sad sigh: "You guys look ready to go and do some swimming in the Sahara."

Chapter 6. Getting Out of Stalemate

Once in London, David did not feel like meeting anyone for a whole month. He was not keen to reconnect with his old group of friends – he was not sure if he could even call them this way. He kept busy looking for an apartment to rent and setting everything up for Dina. Past all the hurdles and the doubts, it looked like things were finally coming along – his great comeback and the beginning of their grown-up life, rolled into one. This was no time to sit and chat. All the same, a paralysing dread was gripping him each time he thought about how he had gotten here. What could be waiting for him in return for this shiny new job with its shiny new paycheque? It was a stultifying feeling, like running on shifty, sinking sands. Until, one day, he remembered Tony. "The old guy is just about the only face I could fathom seeing right now".

The first time he'd met Tony was in 2008 at a Four Nations' Chess League weekend outside of London. The "four nations" were, of course, England, Wales, Scotland and Northern Ireland. "Imagine Canada bringing separate teams for Québec, Ontario, British Columbia, and Alberta! That's how the Brits win their soccer cups, too – they're four when all the rest are one," David thought at the time. Tony was an International Chess Master playing for Wood Green; given how good the team was overall, his place was on their bottom board or sometimes as reserve. He must have been in his early 70s and ageing well, in chess and otherwise. He was still taking risks over the board, pulling old tricks out of his hat, and holding his own against the junior players, who were everyone's bane with their fast, impossibly sharp, booked-up moves. David's team was struggling not to drop from the First League. The captain strategically placed David on the bottom board, certain he would score a much-needed win. But, despite his best efforts against Tony, he could not manage more than a draw with White that weekend.

They faced each other in the next season – this time Tony won straight up – and once again, during David's last tournament in the UK. It was early March – the March after Valentine's Day in Sloane Square. David won that game, with Black. He remembered vividly every move over the board and every detail of the tournament, not least because it was the first time in months when he felt good about himself. The silver lining of being without a job that month – if he was hard pressed to find one – was his return to chess. He dove into it with oblivion, as he used to do in his teenage years. Only this degree of passion and compulsion could take the edge off his anguish at the time. But also, there was something about the sequence of defeat and comeback played out, over and over, in the safe setting of a game. It brought about a sense of mastery over the outside world, which was much needed when he was otherwise so disconnected and diminished. After being laid off in February, David devoured Dvoretsky's book on endgames, something he'd been meaning to do for years. When he played Tony again, he could tell he finally impressed the old man. They spent one hour poring over the game in the analysis room. "See, here, I was almost certain I caught you in a stalemate," remarked Tony ruefully, "but now here …" he said moving the bishop, "you managed to get yourself out of it. One clever move – how come I couldn't spot it?" "You were under time pressure," answered David chivalrously. "I guess I was

… Anyway, you live in London, right? I'll give you a ride. I live in Finsbury Park, myself; we should meet for a beer one day. I'll introduce you to my friend."

He had not seen Tony since then, in or out of the Leagues, but now the time was right. David gave himself a couple of days to make sure the desire to meet another person was still there, then picked up the phone. Tony sounded genuinely happy, albeit surprised to hear back from him after more than a year. They set a time and a place close to Tony's home, and David reminded him to bring along his friend.

The pub in Finsbury Park was filled with families gathering for their Sunday roast. The first week of June had been morose and rainy, but this was a bright day for a change. The sun rays bounced off the pub's rooftop, dancing around the courtyard and the trees, landing on the wooden tables, where they alchemised the mix of water droplets and dust particles into gold specks. The three men picked the smallest and tidiest table, half hidden behind an old white lilac tree. As they took their seats around the table, a rush of late-blooming petals fell down quietly. The older men dusted their hats delicately. David breathed in the barely-there fragrance of lilac after the rain. There was a weightlessness about the day, an ineffable presence. Around him, the colours were illuminated from within, and contours were suffused in light. People, tables, trees were all immersed in a giant, live Impressionist painting. It felt dizzying for a little while, but David was not scared of his dizzy spells anymore. They did not trigger migraines as they used to do before. Rather, he now regarded them as signals. Sure enough, the haze dissipated, leaving behind a state of enhanced clarity. "This is going to be a very good afternoon. This, around us, is … Grace."

When Tony introduced him to his friend Saul, David felt thrown back in time and space to the Jewish community of Plamondon. Saul was a great admirer of chess and chess players and told him all about the sleepless nights he'd spent watching the Spassky-Fischer saga in '72. "I loved every minute! But I never had the spark myself," he added with a regretful smile, "not like you and Tony here. So, I coach chess instead – it gives me something to do in my retirement." "And a bit of pocket money, I would think," added David. "You think wisely, my boy!" Saul was ebullient and monopolised the conversation, while Tony was content listening, quietly amused, stroking his long grey beard. The relationship between the two men was clear to David. As clear as the fact that Saul was quite taken with him. "God help me," he thought, "I can barely get along with one father, what shall I do with three?"

After finishing his second pint and getting "Mazel Tov"-ed for the third time, David found it wise to strategise his exit. But Tony was not a Chess Master for nothing. "One more thing and we're letting you go," he said with a knowing grin. "Saul, you had something to ask David – right?" "Oh yes, but see, I don't know if that's convenient for you. You'll probably need to have a look first. Point is, we're heading for a trip to India until next Spring. Since the Elections, we have been too depressed to plan for it – but it is now or never." Saul launched into a political diatribe; both he and Tony were staunch Labour voters. They looked a little disappointed by David's lacklustre reaction. "You Canadians are so tame – where is your passion?" "We've lost it all when we adopted our famous liberal values," joked David. "I'll say – Liberalism in England is the funniest beast. Historically, it's been almost non-existent, despite what we have seen in these elections. The country is too polarised, too socially ossified to have capacity for a political middle ground in any meaningful way. But we still have the passion – at least our old, embattled generation. We'll never get jaded of politics, me and Tony and our friends. We've been driving ourselves crazy throughout the elections last month – the TV debates kept us all glued to our seats. And then the counting of the votes … and the result! I didn't see it coming, though Tony here did. But I just feel it in my bones the Tories are going to truly and irreversibly take Britain to its grave. The wealth gap is getting wider and wider; the country is still weakened by recession. Labour would have rebuilt it eventually. With sacrifices, austerity perhaps, but they would have – they've done it after the war." "I think we can all agree it's not the same Labour party," observed Tony. "Nonsense! It's the principle, the mindset. It's thanks to them anyway that our banks haven't shared the fate of the American ones when the Crunch hit, is it not? David, you can correct me on this." David knew better than to argue with the elders, and, in fact, he suspected Saul was broadly right. Seeing as his passion was not shared within the group, the old man relented. "Well fine, maybe I am a little subjective, a little out of touch – but is Cameron the answer we've been waiting for? Do we need more Eton boys telling us how life in Britain really is?" Tony made an impatient gesture and Saul took his cue. "So, anyways … 'retournons à nos moutons', isn't it, David? Tony has asked his nephew to check in on his apartment while we are away, but my studio in Canary Wharf is going to stay empty. You've told us about how you just found a good place in London; you're bringing your girlfriend too – Mazel Tov! I just need someone to come in every couple of weeks or so, make sure things are in their place, no issues with the heat or water, the neighbours, that sort of thing. Of course, we're not expecting an answer right away; you'll need to see the room, like I said, and …"

A room. The room. *His* room. The physical and mental space to ponder his next move, get himself out of stalemate. And maybe, a room where he could dream. "Actually, Saul, it's a yes. I don't need to see anything; I just know I'll be fine. Don't forget to give me the keys when you guys leave." "Why, thank you, David, my boy. That was quick – Mazel Tov!"

Chapter 7. Pub Psychology

David was not one to shy away from leading, and not just at work. But, whenever he was bossy at home, he locked horns with Dina, whose own feisty streak had come to fore after a year together. Keeping the peace was a new experience for David. As an only child, he had not exactly been spoiled by his parents, but he effortlessly took centre stage most of the time and was in charge of the family agenda. Not so with Dina; yet, David was a quick learner, and peace was just as effortless to him as getting the attention. He would have made a benevolent king, he sometimes declared to Dina's amusement – a fair king, one who took an interest in his subjects. But until such a time, he had to content himself with being young David face to face with the corporate Goliath. At least in his new role as a team leader, taking charge was encouraged, required even – and he relished the chance.

To better know each other as a group, David scheduled plenty of team meetings, which he presided over with some pleasure. He held the so-called 1 to 1's with both his Quants and wrote down goals and milestones for each of them, then put together a report for his new boss. Andrei appeared to be the hands-off type; he looked easy to please but also easy to annoy. He did not query or critique the report, and David had the distinct impression he had not made it past the first page. "All the greater the accomplishment," he concluded, "I have successfully managed to avoid the KPIs". The mere sound of "key performance indicators" made him a little nauseous as they were ultimately tied to people's salaries, something David had no intention to play with. Besides, performance metrics were Laurent's speciality. Laurent had been with the company since before the Recession and seemed very much at home. Deliberate and analytical, he had the look of a Strategist, including the right amount of nerdiness. However, David was surprised to learn he was working on the Trading floor, where he had one of the fanciest desks. In fact, Laurent acted as a shuttle between the two groups and had a quantum mechanical ability to be present in two places at the same time.

A couple of months into the new job, David figured he had met everyone within his team. Until one day, when they were all sitting around the table for their Monday morning meeting, and a young woman came into the room. She mumbled an apology for being 5 minutes late, and quietly took the only chair available, the one in the corner. "Hi, I'm David," he said and smiled, motioning her to move closer to the table. The woman stayed put and did not say anything back, so he had no choice but to carry on with the meeting. It wasn't a particularly interesting meeting, but at least it was just them – the Quants – without Laurent and his budget planning monologues. What a majestic group photo he would have taken of this bunch! Seated to David's right was the Senior Quant, Murray, a British man in his late 50s. David envied him for his sense of style and admired him for his level head – he was their rock. The Junior Quant, Rory, was the salt and pepper of the group. Restless in his seat and looking bored 90% of the time, he spent the rest of 10% watching one person or another with an insane focus, then saying something verging on the inappropriate but unfailingly funny. David could not decide if Rory had grown up a genius or a problem teenager in his native Yorkshire, so he landed on "a bit of both". Sandwiched between the two men was none other than Clarissa. Yep – he had to see her every week! Diane had not exactly lied to David during the interview, though she had hidden half the truth: Clarissa did not work directly with him … except when she did. Out of the corporate world for not even two years, and he had forgotten the amount of lying allowed here, especially when they were trying to hire someone. Clarissa had a fancy new title, "Consultant Strategist" or some such, and, albeit not technically part of the group, she was attending all their weekly meetings. This was an altogether different Clarissa though. Her comments were helpful most of the time, her tone composed. None of her usually dramatic entrances and exits, no innuendos or knowing glances. Erstwhile tinged with romantic tones, her moods were flat now, and her looks were plain. Even her outfits were different … sober; this was the word for new Clarissa. She looked like she was back from some sort of rehab – you could just about guess there was something underneath, a hint of past struggles … of trauma. "Oh yeah, the trauma … *my* trauma, actually! Clarissa makes it impossible to tell whether she is the persecutor or the victim. It really is that twisted, her whole spiel. Look how she gives off this wounded deer vibe; poor Murray, he has bought it." Then there was their intern, Wei, an Applied Maths student from King's College. Wei was wise enough to always sit to David's left, across the table from the trio, whom he observed discreetly. He soon became very adept at dodging Rory's jokes – mostly directed at his dating life, or lack thereof. "This fellow will get places by pretending he doesn't understand sarcasm. British people love to think of foreigners as socially inept – it's such a useful card to play when the time's right. And, unfortunately for Wei, the time is always right in our group meetings." And now, of course, they had the woman with no name. A true collection of characters, concluded David – starting, of course, with himself …

David's reflections on human nature were swiftly curbed. The discussion became very technical very quickly. And for a good reason too: the pricing library had undergone a major re-write to make the most of the new multi-core processors purchased for their team. Murray went to the heart of the problem: why was the new library crashing when it was supposed to improve performance? Some fuss ensued around the table, but no clear answer emerged. Rory made a wild guess about the multiple threads trampling over each other's data, while Wei pointed out that too much of the old code was being kept around, bringing its well-known problems. Clarissa sighed with an air of resignation: this was part and parcel of life in the Quant group, wasn't it? The newcomer let the men talk for a while, allowed Clarissa her little moment, then intervened in a mellow but assured voice: "We don't know what the cause is, and won't know for a while. This is because all tests we're currently running are old tests we used before the re-write. I can put together a batch of new tests, specific to this new functionality. Then we can get an idea of what the problem is." "Great stuff!", exclaimed Murray, "I like that very much. How soon can you get to it?" "Not until next week, I'm afraid," replied the woman with an apologetic tone. "But I could log any issues I find along the way and pass them to the programming team in real time." David was pleased with this outcome. He was also keen to move to action, so he wrapped up: "Well, team – the plan makes sense to me. I am relieved there is a fix on the horizon." Murray nodded in agreement, not without a small frown of disappointment at the pace of the proposed changes. However, he and David seemed to be the only two people in the room listening to what the woman had to say. The rest of the team looked disoriented, as if she did not quite belong there, and squinted as if her slight accent made her words incomprehensible. Though, for the most part, they were just staring at her lips – including Clarissa, for crying out loud.

"Who was this?" David pulled Rory aside after the meeting. "Oh, she? She's nobody, really. Her name is Bogdana." "How come I haven't met her before if she's in our team?" "She's been away this summer. She has a young son and nobody to leave him with over the holidays, so she takes unpaid leave for weeks on end. It took her a while to be allowed this kind of leave. I mean, look at the rest of us – we don't get more than two weeks at a time. Eventually, it was all arranged with big Strategy boss. Anyway, she won't be talking to you any time soon, mate – she is reporting into him." "What – to Andrei directly? Like Clarissa?" "He's taking all the ladies, isn't he? But not exactly like Clarissa … if you see what I mean." Rory continued, undisturbed by David's involuntary shudder of discomfort: "She is Andrei's mistress, of course." David frowned, this time on purpose. A word like "mistress" was not something one could hear in a North American office. Then he decided to keep himself in check: "What do you know, Dorothy, we're truly not in Kansas anymore," he told himself. Then loudly to Rory: "You sure about that? She doesn't look the type to me." "I feel for you, mate, you want to be our team leader but you're so utterly clueless. Did you *see* her?"

During his years in Britain, David had realised that Eastern Europeans had a special status here, and not in a good way. The latest newcomers from an already suspicious-looking European Union, they were a tolerated species. Women in particular were overly sexualised, seen as cheap, vulgar – and desirable. A toxic mix belying toxic tastes. David did not like that one bit, especially inside his team; he often wondered how his father would have felt about it. Growing up in Québec, he had not seen this side of the immigrant experience and neither did his friends or classmates. There were differences, biases even, but not overt or nasty. "I'd have to ask Dina," he told himself. "She knows a thing or two about women from immigrant families. She wouldn't be the passive type though. I bet she would talk back and fight her corner if she were in Bogdana's shoes. But who am I to judge? She's never been in this position, and I'll make sure she never will be. Besides, she did say once she had developed her own survival mechanisms. Survival must be twice as hard for women."

Before the next team meeting, David moved the chair from the corner to the main table. It did not get moved back. A few weeks later, when Andrei was away on a business trip, David was given a leave of absence form to sign on his behalf. It was for Bogdana; her son was travelling to Stratford-on-Avon to attend a literary competition for primary school pupils. She came to thank him the next day, causing a minor stir in the open-plan office; she hardly ever walked anywhere or talked to anyone. Her son had won the silver medal, she announced, and David could not help but notice her eyes tearing up a little. He smiled to her again; this time it was reciprocated. "Andrei's mistress, my ass," he thought after she left – "this is a trapped woman. A single mum, she probably needs continuous proof of employment to apply for a Blue Card or some other piece of paper they need in Britain. Hey, *I* am tied to my work permit, and I am from great liberal Canada. She either plays this parlour game or it's back to Eastern Europe for her. Of course, her boss, coming from the same part of the world, knows it only too well. Andrei is not a rotten guy, but he is not exactly a knight in shining armour. He is looking for ways to boost his alpha male image, like most guys in the office. And what about me? I believe I'm doing fine so far! I'm staying true to my benevolent King David, the boy with a handful of subjects – all of them willing." For the first time in a couple of years, he was satisfied with both his private and his public personas – and they were fairly congruent with each other. No small achievement for a 30-year-old. As he concluded his internal pop psychology session, the smile on David's face widened, circling his eyes. That same instant, he caught a glimpse of Rory across the desks, following Bogdana's silhouette with a dejected look. And then it dawned on David: the boy from Yorkshire, who'd never had a weakness for anyone, was developing a massive soft spot for Bogdana.

***

Rory was extremely observant of people in general; he may have fooled others with his slumped posture and irreverent yawning, but he did not fool David. After the first few team meetings, Rory started to pay David a special kind of attention, as if trying to decipher a puzzle. With his pitch-black, opaque eyes, and that unflinching stare of his, Rory would sometimes glance from behind his screen for seconds on end, which seemed like minutes to David. Not that he was staring back, of course. But he could feel Rory's gaze, sharp like a laser pointer, always landing in the same spot, mid-way down from his hairline to his eyebrows. Once in a while, to defuse the atmosphere, David would make a joke or at least attempt one. He knew his jokes were kind of lame, except for those involving wordplay, where he did a bit better thanks to Dina. But they did seem to amuse Rory nonetheless, at least judging by the flicker of his fixed, feline eyes. Given how irritable and bored he usually acted in the office, amusing Rory was a victory in its own right. David knew it; he knew that Rory knew it too, and that he was, in fact, gifting him the amusement. "I must have sparked his curiosity for some reason. He might be trying to get friendly with me," David surmised. "Like a cat – a big, agile tomcat – never really coming to you of his own will, waiting for you to try to pet him, then walking away. And, minutes later, he might be so gracious as to allow it, just for a second, after which he'd run away to his own tomcat business, which I'm guessing involves a lot of chasing the ladies." David knew he was good at reading people, but he had nothing on Rory – of that, he was sure. "How come he is so young, yet so clued in? He must be, what, 22–23? Freshly out of his big Honours Programme – how could a guy like him even get into that kind of programme, let alone complete it?" David admonished himself: "God, I'm such a snob! An intellectual snob. Why would I think Rory can't be an academic because of his super working-class roots? Roots that he never, ever talks about. Why would that be?"

The truth was that, even though he found Rory a bit eccentric, David was mesmerised by him. There was a refreshing directness, an in-your-face, unapologetic brazenness about the boy, which Rory seemed to be in full control of, like everything else about himself. Never too loud, and never pointless. But, most importantly for David, Rory was intelligent – to the far tail of the bell curve, in his estimation. Rory preferred to learn on the job but would also read the documentation and digest it while doing so, and would reply to David's emails almost instantaneously. He was fast in all his moves, both physically and mentally. "He wouldn't make a good chess player, though," David observed with some satisfaction. "He likes to see himself as this deep, strategic thinker, but when it comes down to it, the boy can't wait for a split second before he makes up his mind. Though this may be more of a stereotype than I care to admit. What did psychologists call it in the marshmallow experiment, the one involving a bunch of little kids – 'delayed gratification'? As in, the kids who abstained and waited for half an hour would get two marshmallows instead of one. And, when the study investigators followed them twenty years later, they apparently turned out to be the most successful of the group … as if 'success' can be universally and a priori defined. What a lot of hogwash! I've always started with dessert and ended up a National Master – Mum liked to say so herself. Though, maybe, if I had waited for said dessert, I'd be a Grandmaster by now. Psychology is such a pseudo-science," concluded David. "That doesn't make it less fascinating though."

Fascinating – that was the word: Rory was a fascinating creature. He acted like a stand-up comedian who might have missed his calling, but not his timing. His laugh was never whole-hearted, yet he had a knack for being entertaining and entertained where others would have been repulsed or fearful. "I bet he'd say yes if I asked him out for a pint. It's got to be beer with this one; if I tell him about wines and what we drink in Québec, he'd probably laugh in my face, call me a sissy or some other word he and his mates from Hull have coined for it." Not that one could really get upset with Rory – he was not serious about anything, never allowing himself to go all the way in arguments. But what Rory had not seen yet was David's competitive side. "He finds me this naïve, goody-goody mamma's boy. If I manage to make him let his guard down, I've won. At least the first round is won – we'll see what move he chooses next." So, he emailed Rory a one-liner. The answer came in less than two seconds – he *was* fast.

They were on: a week from now, next Friday after work, the shabby Wetherspoon's across the street. David smiled from his desk – a wide, visible smile meant for Rory. Then, a text from Dina popped up: it was getting late, and they had tickets booked for the West End – an Agatha Christie whodunnit, Dina's choice. David wrapped up his work, sent the last couple of emails, said bye to the group, and made his way out. Out in the corridor, he remembered the office plant. It was an ugly plant, a large, untidy living thing disposed of by the Traders and somehow inherited by the Quants. His colleagues were so neglectful, they'd leave it without water over the weekend. He came back running, with a mug in his hand. "I've got to water it," he mumbled to himself. "No, you don't." He didn't realise Rory had heard him. Rory the tomcat, with his sharp eyes and ears. "You came back for it because … because you have a conscience!" he exclaimed. Was that the first hint of emotion he'd ever gleaned from Rory? "Of course I have a conscience, you weirdo. Have a good weekend!"

When they met the following Friday, Rory showed up without his default laissez-faire, vaguely amused attitude. He looked distracted; his gaze had lost its focus – there was a murkiness, a turbulence underneath. "I am intimidating him." Because he saw such things so clearly, David tried his best to put people at ease. That's how he managed as a team leader – that, plus his analytic brain. It looked like he was going to need both tonight. "God, it's so noisy around here! The whole of Chelsea has come to our pub," he grumbled. Rory did not reply; he looked around, as if worried by the mass of people. Sensing his discomfort, David continued chatting. He'd noticed the best way to bond with Rory was through a good whining session: "Look at these fools, standing in the middle of the street as if it's Jubilee Day or something. Better head to the back garden." Rory nodded and followed him quietly. They found a wobbling bench. It was a lingering, patient sunset, the kind of sunset David had come to like about Britain. In Canada, days were quickly melting into darkness at this time of the year. Here, he knew he'd be able to see Rory's face for at least a couple of hours longer – and he needed that if he was to make a winning move.

"So, we're not too far from your campus at Imperial College here?" He had to start somewhere. "Sure we are; that's in South Kensington, mate". "Oh, right – I'm mixing it up with Wei's university." "No, you're not; King's couldn't be more different. You're bloody clueless about London in general." "That I am," acknowledged David peacefully, "that I am. You're not in a hurry today, are you?" "No, I'm good," Rory replied, "why are you asking?" "Well, I noticed on some days you look pressed for time." "Ah, those, yeah … I have appointments." "Girls?" risked David. "Nah … it's … it's a therapist chap, actually … though I do have some girls I see later." "Some? Blimey! As in, a couple, a handful? Your personal fan club?" "Don't be a knob, mate." David had to search the word "knob" in the dictionary the day after. It described a part of the male anatomy, though it was not clear if the term was specific to Yorkshire; it might have had a nationwide circulation.

"Look, Rory – you know you're a smart guy, right? Like, way smarter than others. And not just in a bookish way; you are perceptive, agile." Rory nodded calmly, and David felt better. He did not like the socially anxious Rory one bit, and not because he was overly compassionate, though he did feel for Rory – underneath the bravado, the guy looked so lost at times. He didn't like it because he sensed there was a side to Rory that could become dangerous if provoked. "You were right to apply for the Junior Quant role; this is the kind of job in which you can expect to do some modelling one day. A bit of advanced maths, Imperial College-style. No more Excel spreadsheets, eh?" "And when might we see that happening … eh?" Good! He had the witty repartee from Rory, with "eh" included; things were going in the right direction. David did not mind it when people made fun of his Canadian "eh" – in fact, he made sure he did not forget his "eh"-s; they were endearing. "Well, you've been here for a few months – wait for a year and you could be promoted to proper Quant. And then you can negotiate your projects a little – the kind of work you're willing to do, the people you'd like to work with … I'll still be your team leader, you know? If things go the way I see them now, I'll make sure I talk to Andrei, and we can find a more sophisticated project for you. Something that won't have Junior written all over it. Meanwhile, Wei could pick up some of the basic analysis tools and build on those. He is a bright boy; we should keep him after his Master's."

"Waait a second … if things go the way … just which way do you believe things are going, mate?" Suddenly,

David felt thrown into the line of fire. Rory's eyes had regained their focus, his speech its sharpness. *He* was making the moves now, dominating the board. "That's what I'm being told, that the company is in rebound and we'll be seeing growth soon across most of the accounts. I understand this company has never drowned during the Recession. Not only that, but Laurent specifically told me the Quant team is doing better than the rest. I have no idea how he calculated that, but Laurent has a number for everything – you know him." David stopped. He had been pushed on the defensive. His words were falling flat, and he was feeling ridiculous. What did he think? This guy did not want to be friends, not even friendly competitors. "Aren't you the good Samaritan … eh, David? You root for the team; you want people to do well. Laurent?! Is he your oracle? You mean you've never noticed Clarissa cozying up to him – what do you think they talk about? You think people are fond of you? They pat you on the back, mate – but that's because you refuse to see them for who they are. Because you keep making the same mistakes. You're never on the lookout, never punish people for what they've done to you. I thought we Christians were the ones turning the other cheek – not a Jewish boy like you who learnt 'an eye for an eye' in school. But you're worse than all of them, mate. You are an empath …. you fall in love. You fall in love, and …" "That's enough, Rory, don't you think? You don't care about the promotion, fine. You don't care about me caring about you – I get that. But there's no need to …" "To what? Open your eyes? Show you how they're gearing up to scapegoat you? For good, this time around? You can't accept how twisted the two of them are. And not just them; you think the Strategy people have never heard a thing about your past? Yo, this is England; there is no end to the rumour mill once it's set in motion. And there's no better fodder than a foreigner. It's always 'the others', never 'us'. And you sit here, blindly … full of love for the world."

David watched in dismay how Rory's face grew a sarcastic grin, which quickly morphed into a sneering grimace. His eyes turned from scrutinizing to laughing – not his usual amused look but a cruel glee, so unfit for the moment that it made him think there really was something off about this guy. He was being given a preview of dangerous Rory – and for what? For showing him some kindness – and maybe getting too close for comfort. Ok then – time to move back the probing pawns, clear the ranks … protect the Queen. Time to switch on the analysis brain. "Yeah, I mean, some of that could be true. Though, if you look at the facts, the projected revenues, not only by the traders but also from some of our theoretical predictions, we're fine. More than fine – attractive. There's actually an interested party, a consultancy in Cambridge. They're going to pitch for a deal with us soon … and then, we get a slice of the big pie if we develop a model together – a new pricing tool. It would be *the* project we Quants have been waiting for; a way to prove our skills as a group. But you're right, there are no guarantees for any individual team member as such …" David wanted to stop here but his anger was bubbling underneath and got the better of him. He blurted: "Why do you say it's going to be me again? What will I take the fall for? Nothing is crashing down. And what is wrong with f-ing falling in love?" He meant this as an attack but could hear his own voice shaking underneath the words. Rory had touched a wound, one that had never healed. Not accidentally – he did it by design. How come this guy just knew things about people? Things they had never shared, never confessed – not even to themselves. And what was the psycho-empathbabble all about? At last, Rory answered in a gloomy voice: "Falling in love when you're not loved back is pitiful. Falling in love when you're *hated* – only an idiot does that." "No, she never … that's not true – she didn't mean it like this." "Oh, but she did, and you know it, David boy." This was becoming painful. No more discoveries, no more getting Rory to show his cards. There were no cards underneath this empty, mean shell of a guy. He wanted to punch Rory in his laughing, disgusting mouth. But when he rose – they both did, David just an inch taller but much wider across the shoulders – all he could bring himself to do was avert his eyes from Rory's. A wave of deep shame seized him, making him smaller than his stature. Small like a young, powerless boy who had to take it and shut up …

… This was not him! He did not have this kind of childhood – it was Rory he was experiencing in that instant. "Remember this from me, David: when people make you feel like a big nothing, it's them! It's them projecting outwards their nasty stuff, so they don't have to deal with it. And you can sometimes act like a sponge. Trust me; I didn't major in Psychology for nothing." His mother used to tell him things like this when he was young. He'd never been bullied or humiliated as a kid, but he was sensitive, like her. And also like her, he would sometimes come back home from school and cry. Rada understood – painstakingly, at every step, she observed him and helped him grow stronger. Like a plant, she straightened the stem so light could reach it, poured some water here, plucked a stray leaf there. His mum. The plant. THE PLANT. "Because you have a conscience," Rory had said. What an odd thing to say to someone! He didn't even have that big of a conscience … but he didn't have none, either. The plant. The love. The empath. The therapist … the sociopath.

He shook all over, as if to liberate himself of his own visions, but he couldn't. There they were, at opposite sides of the human experience, meeting each other in the most unlikely way. The shame was lifting, replaced by a wave of tenderness for Rory, the young man of twenty-two who had to see a psychologist every week, probably for the rest of his life, just to make sure he stayed out of trouble. Who was aware he was different and lacked something and made up for it by observing people so deeply and thoroughly he intuited who they were at their most vulnerable core. The scared little boy who hit before he was hit and was terrifyingly effective at it. Adopted and Korean, with an astounding intelligence to boot, he must have been mercilessly bullied by the Yorkshire lads. He was in the know when talking about foreigners always taking the fall.

It was getting dark in the beer garden, but David could see Rory's cheeks, sweaty and flushed. And Rory could probably see the stealthy tear in the corner of his eye. They both sat down again, silent for a few minutes. A waiter passed by, and David ordered another round for both. He lit up a cigarette. "I didn't know you smoked." "I don't – not anymore," said David, "I'm just keeping a few cigs in my pocket for those special moments. Like the magical bonding experience we've just had." "Smoking sucks, mate; you'll die." "You'll die too, Rory." "Yeah, but I'll be a healthy corpse ... You were right about Clarissa; she did not hate you. I mean, not when she was lucid. But I guess ... back then, coming from an institution like she did, she couldn't tell right from left most of the time." "How the hell do you know so much about everyone, Rory? What institution?" "That, I couldn't tell you. But she did have a nervous breakdown and was told not to stress herself too much. That's when she quit teaching Maths." "And came to us instead!" David let out a bitter chuckle. Rory summoned half a smile in response, but David could tell he'd put back his everyday mask – the mildly annoying and annoyed young man, the one with an attitude problem. "But you do need to watch your back, mate; I was right about that one." "I'm sure you were. You're quite the psychologist, Rory – you see through everyone, analyse every little move." "It has a name: armchair psychology – or, in our case, let's call it pub psychology. Better sport than chess, David. Saves your life." "Why are you on my side, Rory?" "It's not me, mate; it's my therapist. He taught me to practise doing the right thing and stuff." "Oh, yeah? Since when do you listen to people's well-intended bad advice? Just tell me, man to man: why the heck are you helping me?"

Rory paused, giving him a slanted look that asked: "Do you really want to know?" and then proceeded: "Have you heard of the prisoners' dilemma?" "What, more psycho-babble? I thought we're both smarter than that." "No, listen, this one is interesting. It was designed by our common friends, the mathematicians. Two American blokes came up with this simple scenario: you've got two players, right? Two prisoners. Each one suspected of having committed a crime, but there's no witness aside from the other guy. Each one is told he will get a reduced sentence if he testifies against the other. They have 3 options: (1) neither agrees to testify and they both walk free due to lack of evidence; (2) they both testify against the other and get reduced sentences; and (3) only one testifies, the other doesn't, which confirms the silent guy's guilt. In this case, the silent guy receives the maximum penalty while the testifier walks away scot-free. Why you rolling your eyes, mate?" "There's nothing new with this so-called dilemma. It is the good old game theory. I even talked about it to a friend of mine, Clive. He is American just like these scientists. Funny, for a super-power acting with so much recklessness on the global arena, they're so in love with their ethical dilemmas! And I know how the game ends: the so-called 'rational' choice – the one securing a milder penalty – would be for them to testify against each other. If one of them plays nice and keeps quiet while the other has no qualms testifying, the nice guy finishes, of course, the last." "Correct! That's what they called the sucker's payoff!" Rory was almost excited: he had met his twin brain after all … He carried on: "That's what happens if you play the game once and the prisoners never meet again. But imagine playing out this scenario over and over with the same person: they will remember what you've done in your previous move. So, there was scope for scientists to take this to a whole new level. They let the gamers use their knowledge of the previous moves and, over time, guess their opponent's favourite playing style: 'mean' or 'nice'. Later, everyone was called to make a guess: economists, sociologists, political scientists, psychologists of course – they all submitted their gaming strategies into a round-robin tournament. Some came with rigid models: all-nice or all-mean; nice until triggered, then all-mean; and others with highly sophisticated ones." "Okay, who won then?" "You'd be surprised, David. The winner was the age-old 'tit for tat', where each player paid in kind, mirroring their opponent's moves. The Old Testament's 'eye for an eye' and all that sort of thing – which, by the way, you've been oblivious to until now. And then they took it further and carried out loads of iterations. After about 200 rounds, a 'generous' tit-for-tat emerged as the winner, one in which players became more 'civilised' in time, learning the supposed value of patience and altruism and allowing for a few mistakes before retaliating." "So, what you're saying is that ethics is a product of evolution and not a moral choice?" "It would appear so, mate. It's purely instrumental. At the beginning it truly was 'survival of the fittest' – the ruthless generation always won." "However, old Darwin never equated 'fit' with 'ruthless', but rather with 'adaptable'. But ok, Rory, you made your point. Fast-forward a few generations and you get stupidly naïve David, is that what you mean?" "It could be worse, mate. Remember 'Brave New World'? Fast-forward a few more generations past you, and you could get a complete softie with no balls." "Touché! If I continue to play nice and never cheat, never capitalise on the little amount of dirt I have on people, one iteration after another, the only thing that will accumulate will be my losses." "Bingo! Think financial crisis with a twist: your self-induced ethical dilemma. Don't let yourself caught up in this twist. You stand to bankrupt your life, not just your bank account – and for whom? These guys are not on your level – and yes, I am including Little Miss Sunshine among 'the guys'. I've never been one for political correctness and I'm not about to start today. And one more thing: why are you all so bloody panicky about the stocks falling to an all-time low? Am I the only one who sees beyond this? Buy it, mate – buy the lot of it while the market's cheap, and you'll be rich in a few years' time."

Rory's eyes were limpid and wide now – this might have been the first time in his life when he was reaching out a hand. Somehow, he had allowed himself the ultimate vulnerability of being seen by another human being. A fleeting, imperceptible concession, which he quashed with the usual ironic to-and-fro: "At the end of the day, I couldn't care less what you do with yourself, mate. Your girlfriend is cute though; I saw her once when she came to pick you up from the office. I'd be sorry to see her take the hit together with you. But if you guys don't work out, I wouldn't mind having her join my fan club – the one I meet on Friday nights." "I'll pass it on, mon ami, I'll pass it on." "See, that's why I'm keeping you around. At least you're not a boring moralist like the rest of them." Rory rose, heading to the gate. "Yo, Rory! Aren't you waiting for the beers?" "You drink them both, mate. I prefer wine."

Chapter 8. "Don't Blink!"

In all probability, Rory was right. That guy! So wise and yet so foolish … David did not believe Rory's paranoia was backed up by any concrete facts, but he had to acknowledge the boy had an uncanny people radar. Which meant he needed to investigate the situation. For that, David resolved to work less and look around more. It was a sneaky way of being in the office, one that did not come easy. "I'm so untalented at office politics, I wonder how I ever got promoted … Rory was right on this one: I was convenient more than appreciated. To them, I was the nice guy, the outsider who couldn't see through their little games. Well, new news: I know a thing or two about games myself." He stopped this train of thought. He could almost hear Codrin: "Don't be cocky, Davidutz. That's where your blind spot is. Born in the year of the Rooster, 1981 – you know I don't believe in this stuff, but what can I say? Rooster is what you are – a natural leader, active and confident … but credulous. You take people at face value."

Point taken; he had to sharpen up. And, speaking of blind spots, he started with Clarissa. To his surprise, the more he analysed her behaviour, the more her mystique was dimming, retreating in the shadows. The shadows of that one evening in Sloane Square. But, to her credit, in this new place, Clarissa was consistently staying out of his way. They'd never had a serious conversation, not even a hint. In fact, he hadn't even thanked her for the recommendation yet. She was indeed gravitating around Laurent lately, the office gossip du jour – at least according to young Rory – being that they were together. David was inclined to file this away as a natural impossibility – or maybe a convenient rumour. He could not shake the feeling there was something vaguely asexual about both of them. But, moving on … other than Clarissa and Laurent regularly going out for lunches, he could not pinpoint any goings-on in or around his team. The next task he set himself was to attend as many management meetings as were accessible to him, which he normally dreaded. During the meetings, each time he was tempted to actually follow the content of the presentation, he forced himself to stop and surreptitiously check out people's faces instead. After all, he was good at reading between the lines. What did he read? Suspicion, petty jealousies, embarrassment? Yes, yes and yes. Malicious ulterior motives? Not so much.

At times, beneath the corporate wooden language about projections, risks and profits, David would catch glimpses of a game: the game of who blinked first. Questions were raised during the meetings, presented as pressing issues. People would gather around and talk about finding solutions. This was all a carefully orchestrated dance; they were not trying to find anything. What they were really hoping to find was a hapless enthusiast – the one with the ideas, who ended up owning the problem. With his innate preference for action, and with the memory of his dismissal still fresh, David found himself compelled more than once to be the first who "blinked". It was an impulse that had served him well in school but now was turning against him. Once in "fixer mode", he was stuck, alienated from the decision-making elite, that tiny group within the group who were too busy figuring out "the big picture" to care about solutions.

Okay, he was a blinker and a fixer – so what? Ultimately, these corporate games were benign and did not feed into Rory's conspiracy theories. Until one day, when David received an email from his boss: a new position was becoming available, in Dubai. Occasional announcements such as this were usually sent round to the entire team – this one was for David personally, or so it seemed. "He might have blind-copied the rest of the team leaders," thought David. It was not clear whether David was meant to volunteer for the role or make a recommendation from within his team. He certainly had no desire to do either, so he filed the email away. A month later, Diane, who apparently was involved in this conversation too, emailed him "just to follow up". To "avoid overlap and optimise the workload", now that additional support had become available in Dubai, she needed David to fill in a weekly spreadsheet detailing his projects and the time spent on each one. "It is much appreciated and will support your future performance reviews." Again, no carbon copy – the message seemed to be for him only. David complied, of course, but felt uneasy about it. It wasn't so much that he was asked to justify his time; as for performance reviews, he didn't have a care in the world. Rather, the feeling that he might have been singled out started gnawing at him.

By mid-December, the big company get-together was announced – and, with it, the wrapping up of 2010. They were treated to a 5-minute pep talk by Seamus, the Head of Trading, via video link of course, as he was never in London these days. Andrei spoke for half an hour and mentioned the prospective deal with the Cambridge group. In his 20-minute slot, David repeated what he had told Rory – that the Quant team would relish working on something new in 2011. As he was saying the words out loud, David could feel himself getting more assured by the minute. The meeting was closed by Laurent, who, unsurprisingly, had been invited to share the last budget of the year and comment on it from a commercial perspective. His presentation fully captured David's interest. It was well researched; this guy was not just an ace at image management – his analyses had depth. After pooling the data and looking at it from a few different angles, Laurent ended on an upbeat yet slightly concerned tone – a perfectly crafted combination. He called upon all teams, Quants included, to ensure that "everything was done to improve efficiency across departments."

The end-of-year meeting brought about a general sense of relief. Christmas was approaching with no lay-offs in sight! Finally, people got to spend a worry-free holiday for a change. David noticed his colleagues walking around with a spring in their step, even the older ones – especially them. Those in their fifties and sixties reminded him of Dad – grumpy, a bit rough around the edges, soft on the inside and utterly uncomfortable showing it. For all the stereotype about him having a Jewish mother, David felt he related well to men, more so than other team leaders. He had an easy rapport with older people in particular – the product of being an only child, perhaps. At this time of the year, he felt at peace thinking about "the old timers", who would have struggled hard to find a new job. At this time of the year, David missed his parents.

As the company was getting ready for the Christmas party, the mood lightened up across the entire office. Even Rory seemed to come to life at the prospect of hanging out with people – "a small victory for the team but a big victory for humanity," thought David. Except this time around, it was David who had lost his appetite for socialising. If he was being honest with himself, he had no desire to meet Rory again; but mostly, he couldn't fathom acting chummy with Clarissa and Laurent. Feeling conflicted about Clarissa – that made sense to him, but why Laurent? David could not justify his visceral dislike. He'd found no proof of a ploy by Laurent or an impending foul move, and had to conclude that, despite Rory's dramatic warnings, there was no target painted on his head. The kid had an over-active imagination; just look at the "empath versus sociopath" theory he believed in. Granted, Laurent may have been scheming, Clarissa was weak-minded. But to harm him a second time around, actively plan his demise, end all his hopes for a career – that would have meant a whole new level of scheming. Callous. Not to mention gratuitous: he'd never done anything to them!

But, on the other hand, what if …? What if Rory was on to something? What if callousness existed as a fact of life – one that David seemed to have a hard time accepting? What if his own worldview of nearly thirty years had been wrong? Nah, this could not be. He had Dina, his parents, their friends … there was a whole world out there: a world that couldn't be all wrong. But, maybe, incomplete? "Funny, I can read a sociopath but I can't figure out my own mind." David did not enjoy having these bitter insights; they felt like a waste of time. But what to do? "Let's run through the argument again: I'm good at what I do. I have results; I get along with people. Laurent is always amiable with me, never hostile. He's also quite competent and solid in his position; he has no reason to feel threatened. Though, with his École Polytechnique pedigree, I wonder what he's doing as a glorified accountant. As for Clarissa, she is weird all right, but I'm the only one who knows it, aside of course from Rory. People here have not seen that side of her, and even if they had … she is hard-working, intelligent, polite. And finally, the numbers have spoken. The company is doing well, and we are out of the Recession. Why plan to do a thing like this? And why to me?"

God, this was so frustrating! He simply couldn't go any farther with this surface-level thinking. He wondered how Rory would have judged the situation. "Well done, David," he said to himself, "you're taking lessons from a diagnosed sociopath." But seriously: why were people mean? In self-defence, would be the answer. Then, let's rephrase the question: why were people mean when they did not need to defend themselves? Take Rory for example: why was he so cruel when they met at the pub? He felt intimidated by David's presence, for sure, and by the "empath" construct – which was another name for his obsession with what he lacked in himself. But that was not the whole story. Rory was never vicious to David in the office; his cruelty came and went at his convenience. Same for Clarissa and her so-called "madness". As for Laurent, he always worked behind the scenes. They all did what they did when there were no witnesses around. Or … because there were no witnesses. Because they could control the situation, take charge by aggressing first. A-ha! Well, that was simple … but not easy. *They did it because they could.* They could and they had it in them to do such things without a blink. That's why David had such a hard time understanding them: because he lacked that "something". And that's exactly why they were going to get him for a second time. Because it had worked before – after all, Clarissa had the full story up her sleeve. Because it was their playbook. And because, where David was concerned, there were no consequences to their actions – they simply *could.*

So, actually, David *needed* to attend the Christmas party – to finish his investigation. He'd taken the big mental leap of faith; now, as a scientist, he had to verify. Besides, he wanted to say Merry Christmas to the team, pick up his gift from Secret Santa – do everything he could to look like his usual self. David the human, the irremediably wholesome and unaware nice guy. As if on cue, the next morning, an email was waiting at the top of his inbox. He winced when he saw the name. Clarissa – her first email to him in nearly two years since that fateful night. Clarissa, the weak link. "Xmas party is coming, and Laurent is away on a business trip. Would you care to join me?" "Nice move," thought David, "inviting me as a replacement for Laurent. Don't look her way!" he told himself, as if a powerful Medusa was waiting to turn him into stone. He looked, of course, and there she was, buried into her chair a few desks away – fragile, slightly despondent, forever outside his grasp. She lifted her eyes to glean his answer. "Don't blink! She'll never know." The world stayed in sharp focus, without the daze he was accustomed to. No dissonance this time; no doubt – his gut feeling was finally aligned to his cognition. He'd never noticed the vacuousness of Clarissa's expression until now. She seemed trapped in a perpetual free fall, not sure whether to stay in this world or take the jump to an extra dimension – or to the void itself. From the corner of his eyes, David caught a pitch-black gaze – Rory's. He looked unfazed, or maybe slightly pleased, and nodded infinitesimally towards David. "Don't blink! And go for it." David wrote back: "Thank you, Clarissa. Good idea, let's meet and go together." Clarissa was going to give him the proof. Why? Because he knew she *could*.

Chapter 9. A Room with a View

Life with Dina held few surprises – and that was a good thing. It came as no surprise to David that she'd adjusted to Britain so quickly, and that the weekly phone calls with her parents soon became monthly calls. Since the day they'd met, when she heard him speaking of London, Dina had made it clear how much she wished to leave her old life behind. She knew where she was headed and was never going to make a U-turn. She was no longer a young girl; come to think of it, she'd never been one, despite her starry eyes. That her attachment to David deepened was no surprise either – she'd always let him know he was the one: the one who stayed, the one who listened to what she had to say. For that, she was prepared to overlook the shred of distance that was left between them, the last bastion of David's past.

And finally, one late November evening, it came as no surprise when Dina told him she was pregnant. They had wished for it, spoken about it for a few months. "We can do it, David – I've got a good feeling about your comeback. I'm settled here in London, content. My days are peaceful – certainly, more peaceful than at home," she used to tell him. Now that it happened, the pregnancy became their enthralling reality. They witnessed and recorded every change, big or small, lest they might miss any sign of importance. But with her pregnancy, just like the rest of Dina's life, things were going smoothly and according to the grand design. In fact, David seemed to be more in awe than Dina. Awe at her body rounding a little every week, her unstoppable sleepiness, benign patience with the world, and deep wisdom setting in. Dina would say, almost apologetically: "My pregnancy hormones are shooting through the roof – that's all." "No, Dina. You are a master magician!" And, because he now knew her capable of creating such magic, he decided it was time to bring Dina into his secret room.

True to her nature, Dina showed little surprise when she found out about the room. That was the thing about Dina: she had her own brand of sophistication, of coolness – one that required time to comprehend. David felt grateful to have been spared the obvious question: "Why did you need to keep a secret all this time?" He did not have a full answer himself. He shared the space, the hideout, but not his mystic dreams. Very, very infrequent but unforgettable dreams, which he intended to take to the grave. Or, maybe, when the time was right, he'd share them with his child. There they were, lying next to each other – three human beings in a bed made for one. "It's a girl, I just know it," he said to Dina, resting his hand on her belly. "We'll call her Aisha Codrina." "Oh? You are exceedingly decisive today, David. I thought she was mine too? If it's really a she." "It is. You can change Aisha if you want; I'm keeping Codrina." "Of course you are – anything else you're doing on my behalf?" "Not today. Today you are my guest – and Saul's, I guess. We can get dressed and take in the view from the balcony. I bet you've never seen anything like this before – the wharfs, the Thames. It's not as wide as Saint Laurent, but it is foggy and mysterious. I used to come here just to sleep. The fog above the riverbank is the stuff dreams are made of. And the docks – just hearing their names will make you think of Dickens." As she was getting dressed, he patted her hair gently – that awesomely exuberant hair of hers. It was even curlier in the wet London air. "I hope Aisha has your hair."

They did not make any preparations for the baby in those early months – Dina was superstitious and wanted to wait for her first scan. They spent their evenings going out for walks, enjoying the peaceful, mild British winter that agreed with her so much. "You know what I would like, David? I'd like you to take me to Gibraltar. It should be easy – it's an internal flight from London. We only need to take a couple of days off; no one is going to object at work. And from Gibraltar, we can see Africa." "Oh, we can do better than that! We are magicians, remember?"

They found December to be splendid in Gibraltar. The same sun that was so reticent in England, in this part of the world was exuberant. Fertility was all around them. Orange trees sprang out of nothing, finding unlikely nourishment under the pebbled ground. Dark-green palms reached tall behind the pink stone houses, and oversized cacti did not seem to thirst here. Hand in hand, Dina and David walked down along the sinewy streets towards the azure shore. After a few turns, they reached the very tip of the peninsula, where land, sky and sea merged under the benevolent watch of a giant lighthouse. Right beside it stood the Mosque, equally white and peaceful, shining against the blue horizon. Dina's eyes were illuminated with a kind of happiness he'd never seen before. This was the look of revelation; David could recognise it from a thousand looks. That night in the hotel room, they turned off the lights and watched the ships pulling into the harbour – large and tranquil, kind of like David's clouds brought to earth, gently rocking in unison with their glimmering reflections. The thought of the oldest and most enigmatic of continents being within their sight, sending its messengers into the night, filled both of them with wonder. "I've never felt so close to anybody in my life," whispered Dina. "You are my harbour, David."

They'd come a long distance from the seesaw in Benny Park! And if it took a trip all the way from Mont Royal to the Rock of Gibraltar, so what? David felt a sense of "mission accomplished". With Dina, his actions counted for something, were never turned against him. Discussions mattered, sex mattered, trips led to discoveries – they lit up the space between them with the spark of faith. Here at this southern milepost, he knew: David and Dina would never run out of hope. The next morning, they left The Rock behind and took the ferry to Tangiers. As they were drawing closer to the new shore, the vastness of Africa and the austere beauty of its contours pervaded the silence. They went out on the deck, eager to take in everything. Under the defiant sun of Tangiers, Dina cried. "Don't mind me!" "I won't, if you stop saying it's your hormones. Do not dismiss yourself like that. It's quite all right to cry – it's you tracing a long-overdue trip. And next time, I'll take you all the way to your roots. We'll ask your dad for tips on Algeria when we go home for Christmas. We are going to see them, right? They're waiting for us, all of them – and yes, they miss you too. My folks are writing to me all the time."

***

He knew something was wrong at home when Codrin signed his last email as "Dad". He never did that. It was always "Old Man", "Forrester" (his own translation from Romanian for "Codrin") or some silly name from the thousands of jokes he had collected over the years. Then, strangely, no answer when David called them in

Montreal that night. His parents were always back home by five. Codrin and Rada led a quiet, predictable life: one show per month at Place des Arts; one dinner, usually at his mum's favourite place on Rue St. Dénis. David called Rada on her cell phone the next day; she picked up straightaway. She had news – the time of smooth sailing with no surprises was over.

"I wanted to tell you myself, David, so you know I'm actually doing ok. I had the surgery last week – we didn't share this because we weren't sure, what with the waiting lists and all, when they might schedule me in. I'm at Saint Mary's Hospital, the one where I gave birth to you. Go figure!" Thousands of miles away, her voice was muffled and shaking slightly. "I like my room – it's peaceful, quiet. I wouldn't be surprised if it was the same room I had thirty years ago. Who knows, I might have one of my dreams in here … to give me strength … So anyway, my dear boy, they did take out the uterus, and that's a good thing because they weren't sure about the nature of the growth – they said it looked suspicious. And when they did that, they sent a sample out for biopsy." David could hear her choking up. His knees felt weak; he needed to sit down. "We'll have to wait for the results, but I'm not worried. At least I don't have any night sweats, and I sleep well … kind of. Your dad is coming every evening, but I asked him to carry on with his coaching, not follow me around like a puppy. The kids need him at school, it's high season. So yes, we're out of the woods. A week in the hospital, then up to six more weeks at home until I heal … I'm more or less ok. But let me tell you: my view here is amazing! I can see the entire Côte-des-Neiges and, by the way, we've had our first snow this year. It's all so white and quiet … they turned the heat on big time inside the room; I feel like sleeping all the time. The doctor told me I would feel fatigued and drugged, but that's the least of it. I'm so much better now I talked to you … David? You still there?" "Yeah … yes, mum, it's … I didn't think … I guess none of us expected anything like that," he uttered, putting the phone down on the couch to wipe his eyes. "I know, this one was sneaky. If it is malignant, I'm lucky it was caught early enough. Please don't read up on the internet – I know how this can look, from working at the Research Council. But I'm not a statistic!"

Of course he googled it, first thing after the call – prognosis and 5-year survival data. Five years! Statistics, the nasty bitch. "Dinaa … arrghh!" he yelled from the living room, doubling down in pain. Dina came running, disoriented, woken up, only to find him collapsed on the sofa and sobbing like a child. "She has … she still has good chances to meet Aisha, my mum. She has a room with a view, you know – like us."

Chapter 10. Secret Fountain

It had snowed all day – a dense and steady fall. As the skies darkened and the moon came out, the snow pulverised into a silvery dust, then stopped completely. Large clouds remained amassed atop the city, ready at any time to resume their muted, grey invasion. The contours of St. Mary's hospital were clear-cut and severe, save for the rustling thicket of pine trees around it, which softened them somewhat. The building stood giant, dark and silent, with just a few windows lit. Her accidental fortress.

Weakened but still up on her feet, Rada had a last look at Côte-des-Neiges before pulling the curtains down. On the ground, the snow was fully frozen – a million tiny speckles, softly glistening like decorations for an intimate night party. They soon got smashed under a car that pulled into the parking lot, right under her window. "Look at them! The woman is about to have her baby, just like me when I first came here. They're both so panicked and excited … A midnight labour that will last for hours with no reprieve – oh, how I remember!"

She inched her way to the bathroom. "This is much harder than I thought … but here we go, we take it slowly, gently, … and we go." She was encouraging herself loudly, to no avail: try as she might, she could not urinate. "Oh God, I hate how nothing's working!" burst Rada. She'd never wanted this surgery; she thought a "watch and wait" approach was better. But, of course, the surgeon went ahead with the hysterectomy – out of caution or necessity, it was not clear. "These doctors; they either have no bedside manner or have too much. The secrecy, for goodness' sake – their politeness … who needs this stuff?

It isn't working anyway – I'm not weak-minded enough; I never was. Remember when they called me in for jury duty? They had to send me back home. I could see through the lawyers' arguments too easily, or so they had assessed me. So, in the end, they said I'd be the odd one out in the deliberation room, ruin their process. In other words, they kicked me out for being smart. Well, smarts are not helping now. I cannot pee. It's stinging too damn hard – the whole area is raw and wounded. Hollow. I'm hollow on the inside – half a woman …"

Codrin had requested for her a single-occupancy room. He was wise in doing that – she needed it. Especially the bathroom, which had become her torture chamber. She had the catheter removed but was still walking with the intravenous line connected, carrying around the whole contraption of tubings, frame and pole. "At least I am hooked up!" she mused, trying to forget about the pain. Then, the idea came to her. She'd stand under the shower, turn it on, and have a bit of patience. The sound and feel of water would have to do the trick. First, she removed the hospital robe and folded it with slow, restricted moves. This was Codrin's job, but she'd sent him home for the evening. He did not need to partake in every single instance of her suffering. The man deserved to sleep. Dragging the clunky pole, Rada stepped into the shower and turned the tap on. The water was tepid at first, then warmer, and finally comfortably hot. "Oooh, this is nice! I feel I'm being hugged all over … like I used to be, back in the day. Codrin and I used to love showering together. It was beyond sexual, at least for me; the poor man was as aroused as a man could be. It was healing … a soft, warm, healing rain. What am I talking? Ever since I know myself, didn't I wish to be more permeable, more in touch with Spirit? This is not hollowness: I have a well inside, one open to a different kind of life – an inner flow. It's up to me to find in it the essence of being a woman."

Under the stream of water, Rada could finally let go; the warm liquid trickled down, mixed with the wash. It hurt. She should have asked for more pain medication, but she'd forgotten under the haze of anaesthetics. She looked up, half-blinded by the mist. Above her head, the water had shaped a luminous arc. It was the golden portal of her dreams! That she should find it here and now, in her small hospital room, filled Rada with tears. They mixed with the water droplets, streaming down her cheeks, shaping the fountain she had described to David. "Yes, David, we are loved!" she'd said that night, twenty years ago, when he came to her crying. "Too much love, like too much pain, would make a human cry. Lord, if you love me, please … please help my boy. I don't know why and how, but he's been hurt. Take care of him. He does not pray; he can't see what I see. He finds it hard to fight and easy to forgive. He is all mind, no instinct. The only thing that tells him something is a game." Rada closed her eyes, clasping the IV pole. She struggled to keep stable on the wet floor. She let the golden rain fall, stroking her hair and body. The pain that held her body captive was subsiding. Outside, the sky had cleared, and the first stars were out.

Chapter 11. Sloane Square, Again

As the Secret Santa brouhaha was winding down and the desserts were disappearing from people's plates, David felt a mounting sense of urgency. "It's now or never – but how do I go about it?" Clarissa had been reasonably contained all evening, aside from a bit of loud talking and laughing when she passed by the girls' table. What an uninspired seating plan, boys versus girls – he wondered if it was the old-school lady from Events management who segregated them like this. Clarissa seemed intent on drawing some attention, as in "Look at me, I've got a date, and not just any date!" – but not much more than that. And, of course, no mention whatsoever of having even worked with him before – not once in all these months, and not this evening either. So typical of Clarissa, to act like every day was the first day of her life and she had no recollection of past events or people. Throughout the party, she'd been as determined to talk about trivial nonsense – including, indeed, a commentary on the recent string of rainy days – as only a Briton could be. Not entirely though: her conversation might have been boring, but, non-verbally, she was throwing around flirting signals like confetti. That too was a common theme in Britain, David noticed, to say the proper thing while alluding to something different altogether. Another way to evade accountability, perhaps ... In any event, David accepted he would need to get her outside sooner or later if he wanted any real information. To walk with her again, in the dark ... expose himself so blatantly for a second time ... he had to.

At the dinner table, he could not help but notice the condescending glances and half-smiles on peoples' faces.

Not all people; not his team mates for instance, although they did look bemused by the unlikely combo. Mostly the girls from the Accounting or Events, who seemed very pleased with themselves, sitting and watching passively as if awaiting the curtains and the gong. What did they care about David the person, his everyday life or Dina or the baby? He knew too well from his last job that, for these women, the office scene, the fabricated drama, far superseded the joy of real living. Clarissa had a different mold – her sensitivity did not allow her to be so opaque – but she too looked smug tonight. She perked up when David asked what she was doing after the party. Her evening must have been going as expected.

Outside, the streets were wet and the lampposts were faintly lit and far between. Clarissa's apartment was somewhere on Sloane Street – didn't he know it? So, Sloane Square was his mark and he was going to make the most of this one trip, the last he'd ever take with her. The walk from Chelsea was only about twenty minutes long. He should take care not to look rushed. He had to play into Clarissa's expectation – that he would fall in the same trap as last time and give her fodder for a similar complaint: assault, misconduct, stalking … something. What a reductionist view of people, this woman had. And not just her. "The best predictor of future behaviour is past behaviour," psychologists said; a statement he had dismantled over and over in his mind. One year of experiences, re-connecting with his parents – and with himself – then meeting Dina, and now Aisha … the prospect of losing Rada … in which reality were these to be erased in the name of "past behaviour is the best predictor"? Surely, one had to have some room – and hope – for living, growing, making wiser decisions. Even the stock market, governed as it was by the principle of practicality, warned all prospective investors: "Past performance is not a reliable indicator of future performance." How shallow humans were, drowned in their cheap theories and even cheaper games! Especially Clarissa with her fragile sense of self, who'd found Laurent of all people to cling to. Laurent? She had just mentioned his name.

"Wait a moment, where did you say Laurent was off to?" "I told you a second ago, David, where's your mind at? New York – he promised to close the deal, and it looks like it's happening any minute now." David had never heard this deal mentioned before – all they ever talked about during the company meetings was the potential partnership with the small, hip consultancy in Cambridge. Andrei thought their modelling tool was all the rage. Charts had been shown, some by Laurent in group meetings, where both the Quants and Traders were invited to give their feedback. Everyone was anxious to meet this bunch of four ex-academics who had branched out on their own and put together a fresh modelling package based on the latest research. "Oh yeah, New York – I remember now." Of course, he didn't. "But that would mean we lose the Cambridge deal?" "That was never going to be a profitable deal, David. Those guys were too expensive – spoiled, really. Laurent once said to me that, from their Ivory Tower, they've never experienced the Recession like we did, but feel entitled to the big money now that the bad times are over." "Ha! Actually, he was not wrong, as usual … So, the New York guys are coming along instead, to help us with the pricing model?" "I guess … They're famous for their convertible bonds product – wasn't this clear from Laurent's presentation?" David was puzzled: what convertible bonds? They were not trading any! He'd have to ask Murray later; Murray knew everything technical. "Sorry, Clarissa, I must have missed that part. You know, I've been having some problems at home and I'm a little … foggy, I guess I'd call it. I've been like this ever since … well, for a while. You wouldn't understand. Back to the New York group … I guess they're fairly large? And standalone, no bigger boss to tell them what to do? We obviously do not have an office in New York; so, does that mean they're free to … um … collaborate with us?"

They stopped under a streetlamp. Clarissa looked up to him, her breath too close for comfort, her pale blue eyes sadder than he had ever seen them. "Oh, dear David … These guys are cheaper than the Cambridge group, that's for sure; and the dollar is weaker these days, which works well for us here." "So, good-bye Cambridge?" Seeing the surprise in his eyes, she swallowed her words, backtracking quickly: "At least that's what the rumour mill says. It must have started from up top. Maybe with Seamus, although I doubt he's got what it takes to pull this off on his own. The chap is like a bull in a China shop. Funny how he is the Head of Trading when there are others so much more clued in." Clarissa was making one faux pas after another. Had she had one glass too many? David did not keep tabs and was loath to use this to his advantage, especially with her. She carried on, unaware, sliding down her favourite path: the pity party. "You know Laurent and the boys' club; they never tell me anything. It's like a game to them, singling me out. They're probably feeding me nonsense just to make fun of me afterwards." Her Botticellian features shrunk, and her pale lips curved down in a pained smile. She was actually believing her own delusions! Two years after their walk together, David felt the old wave of compassion – and passion – sweeping over him. He took her arm, just like before. With a newfound fervour, he whispered: “You know, Clarissa, you don’t have to …”

“Oi! Good evening, boys and girls.” Rory sprang from the other side of the street. He had a hoodie on top of the party clothes and looked very much in his element as a creature of the dark. “I would say ‘Get a room’ but I’m afraid the HR department does not approve … would you agree, love?” He gave Clarissa his trademark sardonic grin accompanied by a contemptuous glare. Though barely visible in the dark, his body language must have stung her. Besides, Clarissa was not expecting a witness, least of all this mean Cheshire Cat who unnerved her every time. “Shut up, Rory! You’re what, stalking me now?” “Don’t flatter yourself, love. I’m taking the tube to Acton Town – not all of us live in Zone 1, you know.” Underneath the streetlight, Clarissa’s eyes turned darker than Rory’s, simmering with anger. David could feel her body tensing, gaining strength. He let go of her arm immediately. Here was aggressive Clarissa coming out again – how was she doing it, morphing on a dime? And then he understood: she had no control over how and when she did it. Rory, on the other hand, seemed to almost expect the transformation. He must have seen his share of Clarissa’s growing up. “Bye, love. Hold off writing the letter to the HR this time around, will you?”

So *that’s* how you had to talk to Clarissa. And it worked. The She-Hulk vanished as fast as she appeared, and she went quiet. “I’ll have to say good-bye too, Clarissa, and Merry Christmas. We won’t be seeing each other until next year, I’m afraid. I’m flying to Montréal; my Mum is not well, not well at all.” “I’m sorry, dear David. Send her … my *love*.” She started in a weepy, whispery voice but ended on a louder note, as if needing to hear herself saying the word, imprinting it in the space between them. "Yeah, send her my love," she said again, looking down and clutching her purse as she was prone to doing. Was this compulsion or a self-soothing gesture? Clarissa shuddered, as if feeling the cold for the first time that evening, and steered off the main street, making her way to a small plaza. He recognised that plaza in a flash – he knew its every detail and could feel the old dread rising, imprinted in his bones. Compulsive or self-soothing? Offensive or defensive? She looked back one more time, with eyes that asked: "Don't judge me harshly!" Clarissa had always displayed a funny relationship with words. "Love" and "dear" were generously thrown around and hardly ever backed up by action. If anything, her acts pointed to the exact opposite sometimes. She seemed to prefer communicating with her eyes – she could have had a career in theatre, come to think of it. Or maybe, she deemed non-verbal expressions more impactful but less committal? Just as Ms Warpley liked it … though there was no time left to decipher Clarissa right now. Besides, David was not sure there was much left to decipher. He remembered Rory's story about her supposed hospitalisation, and he himself at times suspected that something more serious was brewing underneath Clarissa's vulnerability. Who cared? She'd simply lost her mystery. She had become an episodic character in his life, pushed to the side by the torrent of events. She probably knew it too, with that striking intuition of hers – she knew there was no point in upping up the drama this time around. Yet, David realised he'd been one step away from a repeat performance of his past, a second huge mistake. And not because he loved her – he did not. It was because he could not stop taking on her real or imaginary sadness, like a contagious affliction of the soul. Was he doing this for her or to relieve his own discomfort? Compulsive or self-soothing? Where did Clarissa end and where did David begin?

He was about to take the tube from Sloane Square when he remembered to top up his Oyster card. "Twenty pounds, please." The man at the counter looked at him for a second longer than usual. "Anything the matter, sir?" asked David. "You look miles away from here," the man said softly. "I was … I'm sorry. Here you are." As he was climbing down the stairs into the underground station, checking his phone with just a shred of signal left, a text popped up: "No need to thank me, knob."

Chapter 12. Wrestling with Time

New Year at home was calmer than David had expected, and less complicated. It was a waiting game, his parents said, and he and Dina understood there was no need to put on a fake optimism. Each time they visited, Codrin and Rada were content in the background, asking about their life in Britain, and this time was no different. Except for one small detail: the centre stage was immediately taken by Aisha. Everyone was calling the baby "Aisha" by now, though Dina promised to change the name to "Aidan" should the upcoming scan prove David wrong. Nevertheless, when Rada was not paying attention, David would try to make a quick assessment. On the surface, she looked much the same, with clear eyes and rounded features; she joked she was the type to put on weight even on hospital food. On closer look though, her stamina had all but vanished. She needed to lie down every few hours – which, she assured them, was to be expected after the surgery. When awake, she acted agitated, spurred by a constant inner tension. She gave no details about her hospital stay and what she'd witnessed there. David took pains imagining the lonely terror that his Mum and many other women were facing stoically, in silence. Instead, Rada preferred to talk about the baby and how they absolutely *needed* her in London to help out during the first year. After one day, her plans were made with the same frenzy that now described most of her actions. She was going to file for retirement, then head to Britain on an extended visa. No one had the courage to temper her impulsiveness. Dina's parents came to visit too, and it was bitter-sweet. Anne made a mild attempt to compete with Rada for the role of "chief grandma", but, seeing as she had two granddaughters already, she readily conceded. And nobody mentioned marriage anymore; David and Dina were finally being trusted to sort things out on their own. Allowed the space to make their own decisions like the rest of the grown-ups but offered help when it mattered. Life's cruel curveballs had put things in perspective.

The one who truly looked changed was Codrin. David's heart sank every time he saw his father's gaunt face and sunken eyes, which had lost their humorous glint. Every few minutes, Codrin was looking in Rada's direction as if waiting for a secret signal. His eyes were busy scanning, checking that everything was fine and her good mood was genuine – and that he was allowed to make plans for the future alongside her. "Men are so pitifully honest," observed David with a sad internal sigh. "They cannot play pretend to save their life." Nonetheless, to his relief, Codrin started to lighten up after the first couple of days. David knew this was because *he* had come back. No words were said, but, for the first time in his life, his father was the one to lean on him and not the other way around. There was more – a peace permeating the home, a calm alliance between his parents, which was new. David could still remember the turbulent patches of their younger years, when each of them clung stubbornly to their equally quirky opinions. As a child, David had developed an aversion to arguments and heated episodes. That's how he had become a pleaser, a dynamic he now realised he'd carried with him in the outside world. As they all settled together after the first week, he tried to find out more facts from his father. The follow-up visits at St. Mary's had been "uneventful" and the specialists were "cautiously optimistic" – that's all Codrin was willing to disclose.

And, for the moment, it sufficed. "One step at a time," David told himself. "At least we get to spend this New Year together."

He flew back to London on January 2nd, alone. Dina was staying behind for one more week to visit her brother and his family in Guelph. On the plane, David finally found the mental space to give his predicament a serious thought. He had postponed this while in Montréal so he could focus on his parents. If he was being honest with himself, he had postponed it for fear of what he might discover. Now that he'd run out of excuses, with all these hours to spare, he played out one more time the conversation with Clarissa. What did she say, exactly? And, more importantly, what did she say of what she did not *want* to say? Convertible bonds ... Getting ready to trade convertible bonds does not happen overnight. In fact, it takes a couple of years to put in place all the infrastructure needed. So, if this was now presented as almost ready to go, the operations must have started a while back … way before David was hired … and they've been going on all this time. Right under his nose. No, strike that, he was definitely not the only clueless person this time around. Right under the collective nose of the Quant group. Nobody knew any better, otherwise he would have sensed some unrest within the team. All the work had been happening not only secretly, but also from a distance. Across an ocean, maybe. Certainly, not in Cambridge. The Cambridge group was the diversion. So, was his team – the London group of Quants – going to "pivot", and provide support for the new line of business? Or were they earmarked to be downsized, phased out, or maybe dispensed with straightaway? And was he on the list – quite possibly the first, again? Somewhere in the background, the leadership team had been making moves on a trans-Atlantic scale – though to what end, it wasn't fully clear to David. As for Clarissa, for all her feigned soul-searching and regrets, she must have been a willing accomplice. The proof? At Christmas, she staged the perfect second act to her betrayal – and nearly succeeded.

A patch of turbulence over Nova Scotia; David fussed in his chair. Half an hour later, the seat belt sign went off, but David's fists stayed clenched. His panic grew. When he had agreed to the baby, after long talks with Dina, it was because he judged their situation as bullet-proof. Despite the move to London, their relationship had remained beautifully uncomplicated – maybe because, unlike his parents, David had chosen not to over-analyse or debate the decisions taken as a couple. Neither of them was foreseeing a return of 2008; the mood was hopeful across the industries. Heck, he was earning more money than he'd ever seen in his entire life – more than his Mum and Dad together. They were on stable financial ground, with no big challenges on the horizon. Until now. The rug was being pulled from under him. What to tell Dina? He had not shared anything with her and was not going to – full stop. After all, even uncomplicated relationships had their price. Still – what to do? If he was fired now, he might have chances to find a new position, but it would still take months. Even though times were better than in 2008, the markets were far from recovered; in fact, David predicted they would never fully recover. In less than half a year, Dina would need to go on her maternity leave, and then they'd have the baby, who would fill every hour of their time.

Time – right now, Time was no longer his ally. It was chasing him, reminding him he had fewer and fewer good moves left before incurring penalties. Here he was, one step away from the dire scenario he'd learnt from Raoul: jobless for months on end, with merciless responsibilities to shoulder. For the first time in David's life, the future was taking on menacing contours. His comeback – their triumph as a couple – was looking like an omen. "Stop dramatising, David!" he admonished himself. "It's simply what people call growing up – though these are not the best of times to grow up in." And then his thoughts went back to Mum and how uncertain and frightening things had been for her. And how, despite it all, she was willing to devote all her time to him – still him … always. "There *is* drama in this – if not mine, hers." He owed it to his mother to wrestle with Time. To question Time's fundamental assumptions – that it brought healing, progress, evolution, with no effort required from humans other than never-ending patience. To question the societal assumptions and resurrect his healthy confrontational spirit from the emotional grave where years of compliance and "fitting in" had buried it. To grab the present by the balls and fight for what was his. He owed it to his parents, and to his own future as a father, to squeeze all that he could out of this ill-fated comeback.

***

Work was starting bright and early on Monday, January 3rd. It was the typical London winter – subdued and sheltered – but newspapers were already panicking about an "arctic front" that was certain to engulf Britain by the end of the week. "It's probably going to drop to, what, -2° C?" David asked himself, amused. His mood was much improved: he'd spent the night in Canary

Wharf, under the pretext he was due to check that everything was fine with Saul's home. He wished to camouflage himself in the foggy air and muffled sounds of the wharf, more eerie than ever at the very beginning of the year. He craved the comfort of not knowing anyone and not being known to anyone around him. And, sure enough, David slept like a baby. His brain fully metabolised the jet lag overnight and was now sharp and ready to face the world again. It felt strangely pleasant to be back – who would have thought? Commuting on the DLR was cool – one of the best things about London. Full speed ahead, in full daylight, not sequestered underground. "I wish we had a DLR in Montréal," mused David, "some sort of urban roller coaster atop the St. Laurent River. I bet I would have taken it at all hours as a boy. Well, I guess the 'funiculaire' above the Olympic Stadium was not bad either. Dad and I loved every minute – I must have made him ride it a hundred times." Every time he left Saul's apartment, he thought of father figures and suddenly felt good about life. "You're what they call an old soul, David," his mother used to say, "that's why you get along with older folks." Not today though. Today, such memories pained him. Ever since they'd said good-bye, his father's anguished eyes and hollow cheeks were haunting him. "I keep getting attached to older people, but they won't be with me forever."

To distract himself while on the DLR, David started scrolling through his messages on the Blackberry, checking what he had missed over the winter break. The usual niceties, end-of-year cheer and budget announcements ("These do go hand in hand, don't they?"). A long-ish email from Clarissa, which said nothing ("She needs to drop the fake tone, it really doesn't suit her!") and, surprise, a disappointingly dull one from Rory with no swear words inside ("Why so coy, Rory – what's wrong?"). Plus, an appointment from their HR manager, Diane, entitled "6-month probation review", with her and Andrei as organisers. This one drew his attention. It was set for Wednesday, January 5th – precisely half a year since he'd started. Ok then, how should he prepare for this little show? Once in the office, he asked about Diane, but nobody knew exactly if she was back yet. In fact, David was surprised to see that, aside from Murray – the embodiment of conscientiousness – and Laurent of all people, who was hiding behind his laptop as usual, the office was practically empty. Wei had excused himself a while ago – he had a couple of exams left for early January – but what about Rory and Clarissa? "That might explain their niceness. They knew they were taking the first few days off and did not bother to announce the team, but needed me for sign-off."

David passed the day talking to Murray; the man had worked everywhere and knew every big name in the field. He was at Lehman Brothers when the Crash happened, and now, two years later, he finally felt safe to share some stories and even crack a joke or two. Only with David though – he was reserved around most people. "What a level-headed, thoroughly good man!" thought David. "Why don't we have more guys like Murray? Why has he never been promoted to management? He's British, for goodness' sake. For all their talk about foreigners invading the country, here is this Englishman, competent and thoroughly decent, and all they can do is side-track him for a lifetime. I guess he doesn't play the right politics, or maybe any politics at all."

David was happy to do most of the listening, seeing as Murray was a fountain of knowledge on so many topics. But when the conversation steered towards psychology, he had to halt it, lest his cries of frustration might scare Murray.

He still could not avoid launching into a rant: "Sorry, Murray, I haven't read this book you mention, 'Britain on the Couch'. I'm really not that keen on couches. My mother studied Psychology and, while it's been a perfect fit for her, I've always found this discipline a bit suspicious. Mind you, by 'perfect fit' I mean that she enjoyed the concepts but never practised any of it. She's been working as a clinical researcher for decades – on the sidelines so to speak, happily so. As for me, I am not too charitable towards Psychology, I will admit. There's so much probing of the mind using poorly defined tools that yield unprovable results. Lately, I have developed an aversion when I realised psychology was weaponised in some organisations – as in, 'this person does not have emotional intelligence, we won't promote them even though they've written thousands of lines of code and put in countless extra hours'; or someone becomes a narcissist the moment the management decides to get rid of him. Am I committing a capital sin here?" "No, not at all! There are lots of British people – especially the old-school ones, like me – who feel psychoanalysis is self-indulgent. Not always though. It's funny how, when you are born into a culture, you have some exquisitely blind spots to it. And, as a people, we are not very good at listening to what the outsiders have to say. I find that reading a good book is a most useful way to get perspective – better than reading 'The Sun', for sure." "Yeah, I should do it more myself. But ... 'on the couch'?" "The title is a bit misleading. See, it's not one of those textbooks that put you to sleep. Nor does it have the pop psychology titbits that make their way into the glossy magazines. I owe this book a lot. It was the first to give me, black on white, a good description of what I'd been doing all my life: racing. Chasing affluence, keeping up with the Joneses. You'd think we all know that, right? We do, but here's where the author strikes gold: by going to the roots, unpacking this game we play. I'd never thought before that social comparison was pre-designed in us – and by 'us' I mean primates, not just humans. For an example, he talks about depressed monkeys." "Now that's a made-up problem if I've ever seen one! Why might those monkeys be depressed? And, most importantly, we care because ..." "Because, naturally, we're all the same. We are genetically programmed to be social – too social for our own mental wellbeing. The monkeys who were low in hierarchy – you know, the betas, the ones who hardly ever got access to resources or mates – were down and gloomy all the time, subdued, lacking aggression." "Give me a break, Murray, we're scientists here ..." "They analysed their serotonin levels! Ask your mum if that qualifies as scientific proof. Our serotonin literally drops when we perceive ourselves as lower on the branch. Like monkeys, we hang out in this one giant tree – of status, assets and achievements." "And reading this has helped you ... how?" "It was simple, really: once I found it could be articulated, my problem became solvable. De-programming: don't we re-write code all the time here at work? We can re-write our mental codes, too. I could continue climbing, getting more competitive and more depressed, or I could sit it out. I had a nice long chat with the Missus and the children ... and we concluded collectively: 'Enough. We have … enough.' Turns out, this is the hardest word to say in the English language."

"'Enough', eh? I like it; it's insightful. It's even more difficult in North America. When I was at Yale, I kept marvelling at those professors and entrepreneurs who looked like Duracell bunnies and had twice my stamina. Later, in Finance, same thing … except that …" "Except the Credit Crunch happened … one unpredictable glitch with the power to wipe off the most reliable of codes. A third of my retirement pot disappeared in one month. It fell spectacularly, right under my eyes, and there was absolutely nothing I could do. The dreams of touring the world in our early sixties went down the drain. We got resigned to the idea of working for about a decade longer to make up for the loss, and have, of course, downsized our aspirations. But, having read the book, I knew nobody could make me feel depressed without my agreement. We took a big battering all right, my family and I, but we still have a little excitement left in us. The Missus had a moment of genius last summer. We were holidaying in Canada, actually, and she set her eyes on Halifax: there are some lovely retirement properties at very reasonable prices. Since her discovery, we're making plans again." "All of this owing to those depressed monkeys …", grinned David. "If I didn't have children in their twenties myself, I'd mind your laughing at me. But I am telling you as I tell them: it doesn't matter *how* you open your eyes – it matters that you eventually *do*."

They both smiled at the same time and eyed the big clock on the wall. It was five already. Murray was preparing to make his way out. Now was the time: "Say, Murray, before you go – did we ever trade any convertible bonds?" "In this company, you mean? Nope; I would have known." "Right … but are we going to, in future?" "I doubt that very much; we have no framework in place for this type of project, and no people … Now that you mention it, I remember I came across a folder on our shared drive, called 'Convertible bonds', a couple of months ago, and clicked on it. It was empty." "Ha! Another prank of Rory's, maybe?" "It looks like something he would do, just to give us all a mini heart attack. See you tomorrow!" David smiled one more time, then sat down slowly, collecting his thoughts. That folder would not stay empty forever. And their very own hundreds of folders and sub-folders crammed with the work on pricing models might be archived sooner than he thought.

David looked around the office one more time, noticing that Laurent had vanished as discreetly as he had appeared. He was alone now, with no one to talk to. David was keen to avoid loneliness these days – it forced him to face his worries about Mum, Dina, their future. He figured he might as well accept Diane's appointment now, clicked 'yes', then headed out to his favourite dining place. Being surrounded by chatter and people felt nice. "This is my therapy, I suppose. I'm social – like a monkey," he thought. It conjured up a funny image, and he chuckled. "Murray would say I haven't had my eyes opened to the futility of it yet. And I'd reply that even wise old people like himself could sometimes be surprised."

***

The next morning, he woke up to an all-white city. A full two inches of fluffy, pristine snow had fallen overnight, and, stubbornly, refused to melt. The weather man had been right after all – maybe without the "arctic" part. His Blackberry rang; it was Andrei. "Morning, David! No need to come into the office today. In fact, we're working remotely for the rest of the week. What? Ha, ha! I know, these guys are making me laugh too. I mean, I grew up in Novosibirsk of all places. And I come here to three centimetres of snow, and find that traffic's stuck and people act panicky like it's the end of the world. By the way, Happy New Year!" A few seconds after Andrei hung up, David realised he should have asked about the probation review. He called back but the line was busy. Andrei was probably phoning everyone in the team to tell them to stay home. He'll catch him tomorrow. Or maybe he should try Diane again? As he was looking for her number, a notice popped up in his calendar. Diane had cancelled their appointment.

Now that he was off the hook, what should he do with his time? The all-white view out of his window was too inviting to spend the day indoors, lifeless and hidden. David decided he would answer his emails, then head out to catch a couple of hours of daylight. At this time of the year, the sun was setting around three in the afternoon, so there was no time to lose! He rushed through lunch, then took the Central line to Holland Park, searching for the Chess Corner. How did he even remember it? He'd only been there once, years ago, at the very beginning of his time in London, on a glorious summer day, buzzing with people. All those chess hustlers, endearing and cheeky – where were they now? "Running away, eh? Cowards! … Only a Canadian would brave these mounds of snow …"

Two Canadians, actually! In a corner of the Chess Corner, there was another one, a second courageous chess soul – Delphine. David remembered her well – how come all his memories were crystal-clear today, as if revived and brought into focus by the pinching cold and the familiarity of winter? Tiny, with doll-like features, Delphine used to play for the Canadian junior team, just like him, but in a lower age group. She must be, what … 26–27 now? One could not tell; she had stayed just as small, with sharp moves – just like her chess game. "Hi there, stranger! You up for a bit of pawn-pushing today?" "David! Goodness – it's you, right?" "Yep – the one and only, ten years older. Out and about and looking for a fellow player. How come you're here all the way from Vancouver? Don't tell me you left it for London to avoid the rain!" "The irony, right? Well, today is certainly not raining – it's gorgeous; I just had to get outside … But what a pleasure! You're still playing competitively?" "No, not in a while. I got a job in London … and then another job … but I am still under probation … long story. How about you?" "I came here to study urban architecture. And I did; I graduated from the University of London a couple of years ago. Then I stayed on … I find this city fascinating." "I don't! You are a lucky girl." "In some ways, yeah, I guess." "If you're an urban architect, can you do something about the layout of the London underground? It's hideous, outdated. Every time I take the tube I feel like I'm lunging into the centre of the Earth, Jules Verne-style." By the time he finished chatting, Delphine had swept the snow off the chess board with the same speed and focus she had as a child. David remembered she was the best at Blitz among their team – and he, the slowest. His strength was in the painstaking, hour-long analyses that gave the others headaches in classical games. "I am so losing to Delphine today!" he thought, and asked her with a smile: "Blitz? Three out of two?" "Let's go, Grandmaster!" she teased, and proceeded to beat him twice in a row. Just when he had decided he would stop thinking and rely on muscle memory, David realised he was winning. "Too easy!" he teased her back. "Getting a bit washed out, eh, Delphine?" "We both are, I guess." She tried to laugh again, but David could tell her cheerfulness was a bit forced. How come she was alone on a day like this? Did no one care for the disarming inflection of her perfectly arched eyebrows, betraying the myriad thoughts behind them? "How did you spend the morning?" he probed, trying to tread delicately. "Oh, the usual … I went to do some sketches at the Victoria and Albert Museum … miraculously, it was open despite the snow. Want to have a look?" Delphine did not wait for his answer; she quickly took out a bunch of papers from inside her coat and placed them on the chess board. They got a bit wet but she did not seem to mind; she looked happy to just show them to someone. An antique portal, an elaborately ornate doorway, a carved garden fountain. Delphine had talent. "Hey, this is Trajan's column! My dad showed me some pictures when I was a kid … it celebrates the Roman victories in Dacia – that's where he's from." "They have a gigantic cast of the Column at V&A – you should go see it sometime, David." "Oh, I don't know, Roman antiquity is not my thing. Their pride in winning, love of technology, and military spirit … you know where else I saw these? You're gonna laugh – in the US!" "I'm not surprised … just look at the Capitol Hill building, the structure of the Senate … all very Roman." "And, like the Roman Empire, the US is now decaying; we're witnessing it in slow and not-so-slow motion.

Before long, someone will come to power who will attribute their downfall to the 'barbarian invasions' – you'll see. By the way, Delphine, I meant to ask you but feel free not to answer … you haven't been affected by the Financial Crisis, have you?" "Me? Not too much … I mean, we've all seen an impact in one way or another, but my firm held steady. We're just a studio, really; a handful of architects and interior decorators … we also had a planer; he was brilliant." "So, you here today … it's just a holiday in the park?" "Um … kind of." Delphine folded her sketches carefully and put them back in the inside pocket of her coat. The two of them started walking along the path leading to the Kyoto Garden. Their footprints were the first and, very likely, the last of the day. Twilight was falling over the milky alley and the small, sturdy bushes. A gust of cold wind blew over them, and David felt gripped by an unspoken grief: the pristine park, the first week of January … the air of loneliness around Delphine. "It must have been a bad breakup," he thought. "It was so bad," Delphine blurted, as if on cue. Had he said anything out loud or was this just another one of the surreal moments of his recent life? "I mean, my relationship with this colleague … the planner … it ended so abruptly. And when he left without notice, I … I had to take a break." "What can I say, Delphine, other than this stuff happens … it happens to most of us. Sounds cheap, I know. The way we deal with it is different though. Maybe it's to do with the fact that we're foreigners and don't have many friends here … we take everything so seriously, get hurt so deeply … and we don't get to go home! We have to face ourselves much more than those who've lived here all their lives." "Look – I am tired of facing myself!" Now he could see the pain on Delphine's face, finally allowed to come out in a grimace; her eyes were dry though, as if she had exhausted all her tears. "Why should I always be the wise one, the self-aware? Why can't I be a spoiled child who gets to come and go as they please, and always has a safety net, a shoulder to cry on?" "Did you try talking to your folks?" "Ha! You're kidding, right? Why were we raised to be so bloody self-reliant in Canada? The troopers, the ones who brave the cold? All I could do was send an email for Christmas, not even a phone call. They would have guessed it in my voice." "I know this too well, unfortunately. Failure of any kind is hardly an option once you've left … a kind of spartan philosophy that nowadays is just inept. The more I think about it and talk to other people, the more nonsensical I find it. There is courage in calling things by their true name and saying: 'Bad things happen to good people all the time; and something bad has just happened to me.'"

He paused, and then, summoning all the gentleness he was capable of, asked her: "Did you get … abused … in any way? You can tell me, Delphine; you see, I understand." "No. Abuse? I have no idea how that would even look like. Or how I would have dealt with such a thing. I mean, I needed to take two months' unpaid leave just to get over one stupid nasty break-up." "Okay … that's … not good, but … I hope you'll never find out what it looks like." He had to stop; in his earnest wish to comfort her, he'd gotten too close to the wound again. Just like in Benny Park. Only this time he was not going to put Delphine on a metaphorical seesaw. Unlike Dina, she was a friend and not a lover – and he was wiser now. "Change of subject," announced David softly. "Tell me, please, what should I see in London that is arty? And not antique, of course." "Hmm … there is an exhibition of Salvador Dalí at the Southbank Centre. It's modern but relatable; I have a feeling you may like it. They'll close by Spring … go check it out."

***

The "arctic front" came and went; life returned to normalcy. All London airports re-opened by the end of the week and David came to Heathrow to meet Dina. She ran to him, a bit heavy, dragging her luggage behind. She had the most charming awkwardness he had ever seen in a woman. "It's so good to be home!" she said, panting a little. David was startled at the sound of "home". He wasn't sure he could make this Dina's home – or that he wanted to. He wasn't sure of anything right now, but Dina was not to find that out. He did not want her to lose that spark of innocent charm. "Oh, Dina, you've missed a major crisis: -5° C for two days! C'mere, you!" He gave her a bear hug. Dina's eyes were as sparkly as ever behind her fogged-up glasses. "Let's get a cab – you must be shattered. I can't believe how fresh you look after a sleepless night!" "I'm not feeling so bad; I managed to drift off for a couple hours. But I am a little nauseous, and a cab would make it worse. I'm fine taking the train – just let me have a piece of fruit to keep my morning sickness at bay." They walked around the airport terminal, hand in hand, until they found the only café open at six in the morning. David needed his coffee more than Dina. She was chatting away about her nieces, her brother, and how dull their life in Guelph could be. "How do you feel about going back to work tomorrow?" he asked, almost hoping to see her mood deflate a little. "What do you mean – how do I feel? Fine, of course. You know Emma called me from England to say Happy New Year? She said they wanted to hear all about my holiday, just as they did about Gibraltar. It's funny, they find it very boring to stay here in England. 'Staycation', is what they call it. Just as boring as I find living in Canada." "It is kind of the same though, isn't it? Life on one meridian or another. Even with people – they all say similar things." "I guess. But yeah, I'm happy to be back. I'll be jet-lagged for a day or so, but I won't really feel it if I'm back in the office. I thrive on my routine. How about you?" "It was so strange to work from home when we were snowed under. At first, I couldn't do any work at all, I got distracted every other minute. I also thought of you … and, you know, of Mum. But then, little by little, I got into a groove. By the end of the week, I had more tasks ticked off than in two weeks from the office. I didn't miss anyone, really – just Murray, a little bit." "The old timer? Is he your favourite then?" "By far – he has more common sense than all the rest together. He is the only one I'll ever miss." What did he utter, what had just happened? A Freudian slip, that's what. There was no way to take it back. He hoped that Dina did not spot it, but she was as sharp as always despite the 7-hour red-eye flight. "Miss him? Why – is something the matter? Are you guys good? You told me the Financial Crash was over." "Of course it is … don't be silly. What I meant was, Murray's retiring soon – to Canada, by the looks of it. He found a fancy house in Halifax. That's why I'll miss him." Great – now he was lying to Dina. And she believed every word, so desperate was she to stay inside her bubble. To live the London life – or rather, the small, pathetic glimpses of a life that she could get next to a guy like him. He stopped himself: "I mustn't think like that. My circumstances may have been pathetic – it does not mean *I* am. She loves me. Look at her – she wants to be my family! She mostly likes London because we are together here. She cannot feel at home in this Vanity Fair – she just hasn't had her eyes opened yet. But, should it not work out, she'll understand the reason: we're not exactly like the rest. We want to live authentic lives." "Oh, David – you want to know the best part? I am showing a little!" Dina rose and turned to showcase her profile. "So, I will have to tell the girls. Now *that* will be exciting! They'll be all over me and, secretly, they'll envy me. Us. They might even ask about our marriage if they have the guts, although I doubt they do. I'll dodge it in the best style ever – we'll look so modern and so complicated … That's it! 'C'est un peu compliqué,' I'll say – and I'll observe how they suppress their stuck-up disbelief. Or maybe they are as sophisticated as they act, and will not bat an eye. You know, I wonder if they'll take me out somewhere – a fancy place, like, maybe, Covent Garden." He smiled – his first fake smile since he and Dina were together. "See, David? We have shown them." "Have we? Shown what?" "You've shown that you are back – they've seen your worth, your mettle. I find it almost Shakespearean – I've always had this grandiose view of you. And, as for me, I've shown our normal, human side. Why would they ever cast us out? They know we're just like them." This was the most gracious checkmate David had ever received – but a checkmate nonetheless.

***

Another week passed. Life on the Strategy floor resumed uneventfully and unenthusiastically, with people still revelling in the post-holiday inertia. The first all-company meeting was set for January 12th. It was supposed to be a big affair led by the Trading group. Only this time, Andrei showed up to lead it, and soon they found out why: Seamus was still in New York. Funny how that happened, noticed David. He knew from Clarissa about Seamus and Laurent travelling to New York, but that was before Christmas. Laurent had come back soon after. Or did he? How could anyone tell for sure? They might have spent both Christmas and New Year's over there. It wasn't like the Head of Trading and his second-in-command had to report each move. If Seamus said "yes", a winter break in New York on the company budget, in the name of sealing the deal with their new partners, could turn into reality overnight, unquestioned. Still, Laurent was back in London by January 3rd. He'd seen him on their first day in the office, before the snowstorm. And the following week? What could he possibly have been doing all that time, home alone and snowed under? He would have been working, just like the rest of them … of course he would…what else?

The company meeting was brief and sparsely attended. Andrei looked out of his depth talking about the bigger picture. He mentioned something about a new business pitch but changed the topic quickly. With Andrei, one never knew if he was deliberately vague or just plain clueless. As usual, Laurent did his bit well, though he seemed in a hurry and skimmed over the budget figures. There was a slight, uncharacteristic nervousness about him, which he tried to mask by telling them an anecdote – even more uncharacteristic for Laurent. It was about Seamus in New York. They'd had a business dinner with an American investor, who came accompanied by some "special associate", presumably in charge of maintaining political correctness, US-style. As they were wrapping up, the associate inserted the mandatory motivational line: "And remember, guys, there is no 'I' in 'Team'." To which Seamus promptly replied: "Just as there is no corner kick in table tennis!" and laughed at his own 'witticism' as he was prone to doing. "The Americans had no idea what to make of it," explained Laurent, "so I started my awkward laugh, and soon everyone around the table was sort of joining in. We'd had a glass or four already by that point, which helped. Typical of Seamus to ruin all attempts at PC talk!"

The company meeting was officially over, but Laurent stayed behind for a few minutes, checking his laptop, then headed sheepishly towards Andrei's office. They closed the door behind and sat down to look at some data together. Only the heads of Strategy and Trading had their private offices, each on their respective floor. They did not get much privacy though as every move was visible through the glass door. "I've seen this laptop before; it's the same one Laurent brought on our first day in the office. Why does he need to use it? He has his own fancy computer on the Trading floor. And what's he doing on our floor all the time anyway?" An hour later, the two were still talking – Andrei in his usual voluble style, Laurent interjecting occasionally with small, deliberate gestures. There was an economy of energy about this man. "He's kind of like a black hole – he sucks the energy around him. Impenetrable like a black hole, too. What do I know about this guy? He never makes mistakes. But he's not a machine, nobody is – there must be something he cares about. At the end of the day, everyone is playing their own version of chess on a board somewhere."

***

Tony and Saul were finally back in London after their 6-month trip to India. David met them at the weekend to hand Saul back his keys. Parting with his "dream room" was simple and without regrets: the time for dreaming had reached its natural end – at least for now. As much as he felt pleased to see the couple again, David was so caught up in his own thoughts and worries that the moment largely passed him by. Saul spoke excitedly: he was already making plans for future trips and destinations, one more exotic than the other. He was delighted to find his old apartment ready-warm and in good order, and did not pay attention to David's mood. Little escaped Tony's eagle eyes though. As usual, Tony offered to give David a ride back, and, on the way, asked him to stop for lunch. It was the same pub in Finsbury Park where the three of them had sat down back in the summer, chatting about politics, the future, and everything else under the sun. This time of year, the pub's courtyard was drenched, deserted, with all the benches and tables stored away. Inside was noisy and crowded, but they managed to squeeze around a tiny, messy table. At least they were seated next to the electric fireplace, which had a large vase filled with roses on its mantelpiece.

"There's just one thing missing from this room: my mother's samovar …" commented David. "She has a samovar? Your mum is Russian then?" "No, she is an original. She'd never be caught keeping a bunch of flowers in a vase, like these ones for instance. You know, they're living things and all of that …" "Aah, she's an empath, then." David shuddered at the sound of 'empath': what was it about English folks throwing around big psychology terms so casually? Didn't they *feel* the emotional charge behind them – the categorical profiling of someone they'd never met, and never would? Clearly, they did not care as much as he did. "She's actually quite normal," David answered dryly. "A bit odd, perhaps, when you first meet her." "I see … she's just like us lot, then." One could count on the old fox to always find the right reply. David sometimes felt like an open book to Tony. "So, what is on your mind these days, my boy?" Ok, he *was* an open book to Tony.

"It is my mum, her health … but there is nothing I can do … in fact, I'd rather we don't talk about her. And strangely, she is not even on my mind that much … which sounds bad, but at least it's a clear-cut problem – definable, you know? The stuff that doesn't give me peace is woolly and nonsensical. Things that happened to me two years ago … and now are back to haunt me." "What sort of things, if I may ask?" "Well, Tony, the sort of things that start with a young lady, a coworker, who wrote a complaint letter as I was being fired … I should be fair and add that the Recession got me fired, not her. But I did get served a one-two punch that was as damaging as it was toxic. *She* was toxic, I'm afraid. She still is … and we still work together." "Oh, my! A formal complaint? You know you shouldn't even be talking to this person after such an act. But you are, clearly … why?" "That is the million-dollar question, isn't it? Well, first of all, I've got to. We are on the same team; I'm sort of her superior but not really – I told you; it is woolly. Not only that, but she was the one who recommended me for this job, which I only took because of Dina, and … and ever since, I'm suffocating. Saul's room has kept me sane; I kid you not. Knowing all these months that I could run away from it all if I needed to … but now, there's no more running. And that's not all. I have this colleague with a theory, that there are big changes on the horizon in our company and I'm about to be scapegoated for some reason. If he is right, I'll need to put up a defence … do things differently this time around. Except that I'm already tainted, weakened … it's like she's got something on me, and she has spread the word around. But she's got nothing! She just acts like she has. And you should see her … she has a face that belongs in the Louvre or some such …" "Believe it or not, I have seen many faces like hers. This sounds like a matter for the police." David's eyes widened. "She *did* file a complaint with the police; at least the HR people said she did. But I have never waited – or wanted – to find out the outcome. I haven't been a very brave man, Tony. I couldn't speak about it to anyone … not even to my dad." "None of us are brave! This is where people who do such things draw their power from. Most of us are a bit like deer in the headlights … we become paralysed. Precisely because we have never done anything like this in our life, we cannot wrap our mind around it. Those in the know are more prepared and sharper – could be this new colleague of yours, if he's as wise as you say." "But then, how come *you* know?" Tony paused for a second, then continued at pace, as if he'd taken a decision: "You're right, I should have told you from the start. Look, David, I used to work for the police. Not as a constable," he specified with a smile, seeing David's surprise, "I was in Admin. But I have filed a lot of cases – some nastier than you can imagine. Your case is baby stuff. The only silver lining to that decade of my life was a marvellous pension scheme – the envy of our friends. How do you think trips like India happen – from Saul's pension as a lecturer? Well, anyway, that's old people's talk. What are you doing at the moment?" "Doing … as in …?" "To get yourself out of this pickle." "I am observing, analysing

… keeping mental tabs on various people, kind of." "Mental tabs, hmm …. what about taking action?" David lowered his gaze, ashamed. "You *are* allowed to act, David. Especially if you are innocent – you're obligated to. What can you possibly stand to lose?" "But what to do? I have no clue about how these things work. I'm in a foreign country – not that I knew anything about police cases in Canada either. Though I do know people need a police clearance for immigration stuff." "Exactly, you are entitled to seeing your own criminal record. It's called a DBS check here in Britain. Some jobs, like those in teaching, require it. I'm guessing yours is clear since it never came up with your employers, but this little piece of paper will put your mind at ease. And then you can be braver, focus on what matters, and go on counter-attack." "Like when we met last time in the Chess Leagues?" retorted David with a faint attempt at humour. "I suppose so. You won that time, fair and square. I'm not going to pretend I went easy on you. You made me sweat and suffer for four hours, but you will not get a second chance from me! Here," Tony took out a piece of paper and scribbled something on it, "call this young chap. He took my place when I retired. He'll help you find out what really happened; I trained him well." "How can I ever thank you? But wait – you know his phone number by heart?" "He-he, you *are* keeping mental tabs, well done! Indeed, I have that kind of memory. It helps me see the chess board better when I'm away from it. That's why I said, when we were talking about your mother: we're all a bit odd in our own ways."

***

The 'young chap' was a stocky man in his 40s, with a strong accent. David was by no means an expert, but, since the man sounded a bit like Rory, he figured he must have been from the North. Also, like Rory, the man had a raw physicality about him – he could have been an ex-boxer or wrestler. "Larry," he introduced himself, shaking David's hand vigorously. The police station looked almost cozy, like an office, and quiet like one too. David had been imagining a scene from the De Niro movies, with constant commotion and phone calls. "Let's start from the beginning," requested Larry. He had the tone of someone used to being in charge. With a quick scan, David could tell the 'young chap' had been briefed by Tony on everything there was to know about his case. Nevertheless, when prompted, he recounted the whole story, or at least everything he could recall, as some of the details of those days were still hazy in his mind. Judging by Larry's nodding and scribbling, it seemed to be sufficient. To David's own amazement, once he got started, it seemed he could not stop. Oddly enough, he found it easy to tell Larry all about the sex stuff. The man looked unfazed hearing the graphic details, though, for good measure, he kept his forehead wrinkled in a sceptical frown. A sort of professional mask, David assumed, meant to unsettle the potential liar. As David finished, Larry waited for a few seconds, then observed tersely: "Your name is here on the complaint, all right. But it looks like they decided not to take it further." "Just to be sure, Larry, we are talking about Ms Clarissa Warpley, right?" "Indeed, we are. Any other young lady we should know about in relation to yourself?" "No, not at all! It's just that you did not say her name, so I thought I'd ..." "You thought you'd clarify. That's fair enough." Now that the story-telling stage was over, Larry's tone moved from reassuring to challenging. David could not help but feel it was all mandatory and well-orchestrated. No mental inertia with these police folks! Tony used to act like this too, switching styles, angles – even his chess moves had this "show me what you've got" energy about them. As if on cue, Larry brought up Tony. Flashes of serendipity like this one were known to David. He almost felt he made them happen when he focused all his attention on one person. "I know you talked to Tony and that you two are chess buddies. But let me ask you something. See, I am a straight man, and I can't wrap my mind about a woman coming on to you like that, in a back alley … against your will." The last part was detectably ironic. Larry continued, his frown replaced by a slanted, doubtful glare: "You're sure you hated every moment of it?" "No … in some way, I didn't. Look, I will tell you that I fancied her. Heck, maybe I still do. But I did not invite the sex, or want it, or hint at it – I did not even think of it. Want to know why? *Because* I fancied her … yeah, I'm that stupid. Look, Larry, I don't have more words to tell you I did absolutely nothing … And that, in fact, it was the other way around: I protested, asked her to stop. I did not want to climax. It felt … demeaning, I guess. Like that was all a guy like me could ever want … or get – the rushed, back-alley special. And, on some level, she was attacking me in the same breath, and saying spiteful, twisted stuff. It was more vengeful than erotic. But yeah, I realise that what I say is inconceivable. Who in the kingdom of God is ever going to believe my story? I am the man – I look guilty by default." "Hmm, I see … the fact is," Larry commented with detachment, perusing the files in front of him, "that no investigation was opened on this occasion." "What do you mean, on this occasion? Were there other occasions?" "Correct; we have a total of four letters filed by this young lady over the past ten years." "Involving other men?" "It would appear so. Let's see … she lodged the first complaint – same claim: assault and stalking – when she was a student. The following were from three different workplaces." "Three other people aside from me? Oh, God …" "You'll be pleased to know, I think, that there was no complaint over the past year." "None yet!" said David bitterly.

Though he was reeling from the shock, David was also trying to keep an eye on Larry's body language. The 'young chap' had stopped clamming up and now seemed willing to throw bits of information his way. He must have done something right, but what? All he had done was to stop caring about his pride and put it all out there. Or was this part of Larry's act, the good-cop/ bad-cop routine rolled into one? Who cared? David was finally getting to the bottom of things and he needed to persist. "Why did you say my case was not investigated? Was there anything different about it?" "Don't flatter yourself, young man. These are all cookie-cutter letters. The lady looks like a serial complainer to me. It says here that only the first two cases were pursued." "How come? This does not make much sense, if they were all identical." "It would appear the allegations lacked specific details. And also, when there's a pattern forming, it sheds a bit of light on the complainant, too." They both went quiet for a while. David had grabbed the desk pre-emptively, fearing one of his blurry spells again. But nothing happened. Larry kept skimming calmly through the notes, observing David's movements from the corner of his eye. "There is another comment here … I shouldn't share that with you; it's confidential. Oh, wait. It's from the last investigator, so it pertains to your case. Says here the lady looked relieved to hear the case would not be followed up. Bit odd, innit?" "Not really, if you knew her." Larry suppressed a chuckle: "I guess you were special to her after all – if you can call this 'special' …"

"I just have one more question, Larry. It came to me just now while we were talking. See, I am Canadian, and when I landed at Heathrow in January, the fellow at the Customs kept me there for a good five minutes. He was staring at the screen for no reason, or so I thought. I reckoned he was just out of it; it was so early in the morning, and only a couple of days after the New Year. Do you suppose that, maybe …?" "This will be on your record, not as a criminal offence but as official complaint. You are Canadian, so you'll need to renew your work visa, right?" "If I still go for jobs in London, yes, that's very likely." "Why would you not go for jobs here?" Larry asked, raising his voice. He looked taken aback and disappointed. "I am not saying London is the centre of the world," Larry continued, "but it's a place to live. Where I come from, it's hopeless for so many. People spend their entire lives on minimum wages, sometimes less. But look around us here: universities, professionals, entrepreneurs from all over the world. Hard-working folks, ambitious. People who want to make some money, build a future for themselves. There's nothing wrong with that!" He'd touched something in Larry, that much was clear. Had David won him over? There was no time to find out, as Larry swerved: "Sorry, mate, I got carried away there for a moment … but yeah, you'll need to bear in mind this incident for future visa applications. It won't be a big thing, but it may come up." "Thank you, Larry – really … you've opened my eyes today! I wonder if she realises how much harm she does to people ..." "Ms Warpley? Look, I'm no psychologist myself, but we do have trained staff here and they've explained a few things to us. What they find with these types is that they're teetering between fragile and volatile." "Oh, that I can confirm! I've seen the teetering in action," David jumped in. "Then you may know you should avoid exposing the flaws in their story … have it blow up in their face, as it were. Some of them, including this young lady I should think, already have an awareness of their problem on some level. But if you spell it out, the sense of shame will shatter them. That's when you'll see their dangerous side." "Larry – why have you talked to me today? And given me advice, and …" "It's simple. You are the only one of four who ever came to us. And now, to wrap it up: I'd steer clear of any attempt to have an explanation with this person. It simply wouldn't work in the same way you and I may sort things out." "Trust me, I won't try. I haven't done it for the past two years … I cannot. I couldn't bring myself to … how did you put it? Shatter her."

***

As Tony had predicted, David left the police station feeling about a stone lighter – and right and normal for the first time in years. He sprinted to the nearest underground station. It was peak hour when he got on the train. As he was standing, wobbling, crammed against tens of other ordinary people, catching their common reflection in the window while the train zoomed through dark tunnels, he realised this was no River Styx. "It isn't shadowland; it's life. That is how people live here – and, if we think about Larry, for many this is heaven. It is a world – no better and no worse than others – a place to be, like Larry said. Larry, my man, my new Socrates! He's more clued in than university professors, so solid in himself, so clear-cut! I wonder how he'd deal with Rory – I bet he'd teach him some common sense." And then it dawned on David: Larry, Rory, Tony – they were all British. They did not push him away or doubt him from the get-go. He was no more alone against the world now than he had been in Canada. "I should stop bashing the Brits. Saul is right: one can't stay out of politics forever. The point is to understand the nuances here. Ok, there is local xenophobia, but it is not a blanket to be thrown over an entire nation. Just look at me, the second time in Britain: I have found allies!"

David got home with a feeling of lightness and was unlocking the door to the apartment, when it struck him: this was the dreaded 'results day'. He was due to call home. Dina was not back from work yet. Her favourite spot on the couch was empty, but he was in no mood to get comfy. He paced around with sweaty palms and dialled the wrong number twice. He felt relieved when he heard Codrin; it was his father that he wanted. "What's up, old man?" "We're doing good, Davidutz! We're fine – your Mum is fine. The biopsy came back negative – she's done, no need for chemo. Right now, we were having a glass of wine together in front of the TV. We haven't watched the news in two months, since this ordeal had started. I didn't realise I had been missing our shady politicians! Your Mum would like to say a word, but I think it's wiser if she doesn't." "Because I'm dru-unk!" he heard Rada shouting. "You are embarrassed with me, Codrin – come on, admit it." "I will admit it for him," David shouted back, with tears in his eyes. "I will admit how happy and lucky we are!"

***

The next day, David received a calendar invite from Diane – the second in two weeks. This one was called ‘Performance appraisal’. “Man, they should give the HR people a prize – the IgNoble prize for literary fiction. They’re never at a loss of vapid terms that sound significant. Twenty-first century creativity at its finest, is what this is.” He accepted the appointment immediately and clicked on the attachment. It was a Word file with a set of self-assessment questions (“more creative fiction”), which David was meant to fill before the meeting. Funny how, this time around, Andrei was not included on the invite. “Hang on, when is this for? Tomorrow, 4 PM. Tomorrow is a … Friday? Oh … ok, then – I *am* being fired.”

Chapter 13. "It Must Have Been a Glitch …"

"You sure you don't want dinner? Pumpkin soup, dash of turmeric, like your Mum makes it?" Dina was bringing out the big guns. "I'm not hungry right now, not sure why." "David, you're *always* hungry. If you've got something on your mind, you can tell me." "That's the thing: I don't know what's on my mind anymore. I'm in a constant brain fog ever since I came back. No particular reason: it's just life in London, I guess." "Brain fog – tell me about it! I did hear pregnancy was contagious. On this note, can I have your soup, too?" "Sure, you can. And add more turmeric! You need to load Aisha with antioxidants. This anti-ageing stuff, it's never too early to start it, you know." Dina was practically choking on the soup. "Stop making jokes while I'm eating!" "Ok, ok … I'm off to my chess board now." "Chess? You haven't touched it in months." "It's funny but I need it now; I don't know why. I guess, with Tony and Saul being back, I don't want them to find me out of shape. I'm sure they played a lot of chess in India – even the taxi drivers are International Masters there." "All right, knock yourself out. I'd like to say I'm tuning into the evening news, or better yet, the History channel, but you'll likely find me dozing on the sofa."

He took out the large wooden chess board, which was collecting dust under the bed. What was he working with here? Lots of sparse, contradictory data, with one clear outcome: his dismissal tomorrow. He'll have to join the dots like he's never done before. After all, he was playing with his future. Strike that; he was playing with *their* future – his, Dina's, Aisha's. Mum's. He blinked, distraught. "Back to the drawing board for you, Davidutz

– the chess board, rather. Let's take them one by one, as Dad would say. Who do we start with? The Queen, of course. Erratic, unpredictable – and, by far, the easiest to place. She comes and goes, chasing the action." Clarissa's beguiling look under the streetlamp haunted him, as did her turning on a dime. "Actually, this one is more like the White Queen and the Black Queen put together. You never know which one will show up." He placed the queens next to each other, in the centre. "Gently, gently, Your Highness. We don't want to shake up Your fragile Majesty. You, on the other hand, have had no hesitation in shaking me up, real good too. A serial complainer, Larry called you. This type of person is a great tool in the hands of those who manufacture chaos. No wonder they won't fire you any time soon.

Next up, the Knight. This guy is awkward; his moves are blunt, impossible to miss. Powerful but not exactly devious. And certainly not close enough to the action." Seamus. He placed the Knight a couple of squares away from the centre. "So far so good. Who is our Rook? Someone who waits for clear passage before moving. Acts super-straight but, when it comes down to it, keeps to the sidelines. Someone with big enough stakes in the game but with less urgency than others. Ha! My boss. He is already where he wants to be: the Head of Strategy. He does not need to capture anything; he's just maintaining his position. If all goes well, he might throw Clarissa a bone – put her in charge of model validation, perhaps." The Rook took its place on the A-file: Andrei. "Yeah, but this guy cannot work in isolation; no Rook does. We need to find the aggressor, the disruptor. The one without whom the charade – because that's what this is, one big, ugly charade – would not have started in the first place. It needs to be a guy who's been involved all along –

before, during and after the New York episode. The guy behind the New York deal. And probably the Cambridge 'deal' as well: the author of its fallout."

The fog was lifting. How was this for a back story? Seamus remained in New York and was not coming back. Maybe he hoped to find a better job in the US, now that the banks and hedge funds were waking up after a two-year slumber. Or maybe he had been advised not to return. The Knight was not an active piece anymore. He was exposed, in clear sight of the real attacker. The Bishop – shifty and oblique in all his moves. Good old Laurent, perpetually second-in-command. You never knew where he would spring from, or when. Now was his time to sweep across the board and take the lead; he'll be the one to trade those convertible bonds. Finally, there was the King to take care of. The King – benevolent King David. There he was, at the centre of the action – but he was stuck, slow and powerless as only a King on a chess board could be. "Where do I go from here; what should my next move be?"

As usual when he reached an impasse in his chess games, David took a break to quiet his mind. He headed to the living room, where the TV was droning on. As she'd predicted, Dina lay asleep on the sofa, covered in the fleece blanket – her favourite one, fiery red like her glasses. Gently removing the remote from her hand, David stood still for a second in the dimly lit room. He should look at her more often, take care of her more. "What kind of king am I? What does it mean to be a king anyway? Dad, Mehdi, Tony and Saul? How did these men become the Kings of their lives?"

In one big flash, the picture came together. Dashing back to the bedroom, David nearly stumbled on the rug.

He held on to the desk and sat down on the edge of the bed, facing the chess board, out of breath. The King. To the outsiders, he was crowned and important; but he was a trapped man. The more one wanted to be at the centre, the more they were enslaved by their own ego. There was no freedom on this lonely square, no mastery of the game – and no escape. And, crucially, the King was not the last piece to consider. He had forgotten! "Here he is, the Pawn – small, uninteresting, one of many. The Pawn moves carefully, removes himself out of the drama, and observes. If he is lucky, he'll make it all the way to the other side, unscathed. If he is able to advance and capture *en passant*, he's a survivor – and he may even get the big prize." The Pawn was in a rush to safety, like David. It *was* David. But David was not the only one on borrowed time. As the attacker, Laurent's moves had to be even faster. He could not afford to strategise forever; the corporate world was rushed and stealthy. So, he was bound to make an error somewhere – omit a detail, leave a trace.

He got it! His intuition had done its job, but now he needed facts and data on Laurent. David knew he was never going to get these through the regular channels. "Rory! He has what it takes to get his hands on this stuff, and I am not going down that path. I may be naïve, empathic, whatever he likes to call me, but I want to stay legit. First off, I do not have the stomach to go further. And also, logically – how is getting into legal trouble going to save my back side? Better tread cautiously, as Larry would say. Besides, so many pieces are depending on the Pawn. But then … who is the King? I don't believe I have an answer to this, and I don't need to. The King is simply the next fool who thinks he's relevant. The guy who takes the fall. And you know what? That's really not my problem anymore; we've just established I'm a Pawn. Tony was right though. I need a simple, flawless plan of action – and I need it yesterday."

***

Diane was middle-aged, with nicely styled hair and a perpetually positive attitude. David used to file her away as 'the soccer mum type'. Her colleagues often said that "Diane doesn't have a mean bone in her body." Remains to be seen … Anyway, he was right on time. Around the office, people were eyeing the pub down the street, where the queue was growing by the minute. Happy Hour was almost there. The irony of that moment was not lost on David. He came into the meeting room holding the piece of paper with answers to the self-assessment questionnaire. Diane was already seated, sporting the serene outlook of someone who was painfully at ease. With a little effort, he could match that look. David expanded his shoulders as he took a seat, and gave Diane a relaxed, though not exaggerated, smile. She appeared infinitesimally disconcerted, so he resolved to keep the smile for a couple of seconds longer. "Hi there, thanks for coming! You brought the questionnaire – amazing. We asked you to give yourself a bunch of scores and talk us through them." "We – as in you and Andrei? Where is he, by the way?" "Andrei is not the subject of our discussion today. I am not aware he meant to attend." "Right – I'm asking because he is my line manager, so it would make sense if he did." "Let's have a look!" she interrupted him, practically grabbing the paper from his hand. And then she smiled again, her pearly teeth on display. "Diane's reactions are a bit choppy today," thought David. "Right, let's see … You gave yourself an

8 out of 10 on technical knowledge – can you explain that, please?" "I still have stuff to learn. There was a lot of theoretical knowledge that I was able to bring from my previous role, but the specifics of IT framework, plus the accounts and portfolios, were new to me. So, I needed time to wrap my head around them. Otherwise, the modelling is fairly basic, at least compared with other systems I have seen. In fact, I have a few suggestions to make on this point." "Very well, you can make them later. You put down a 7 on team management – why is that?" "Well, people management is not something you master overnight, as I'm sure you know. I have a small team, but everyone is their own person. Rory's performance review and objectives are very different from Murray's – and that's a good thing. It takes me time though, dealing with each of them one-on-one, as well as with the group. And then, I have Clarissa and Bogdana, who are not reporting to me directly but are always included in our discussions. They have come up with some good solutions, so it's a case of 'the more, the merrier' in the Quant team. I think I'm on the right track overall; next year I'll be an 8." "Erm … sure. We did collect some feedback from your team; it was quite positive." "We – as in you and …" "I and my new assistant, Milena – she sent round some questionnaires prior to this meeting." Diane sounded irritated but not angry – right where he wanted her. "A-ha! on leadership, I see you gave yourself a 10." "Yeah, I really enjoy leading, and have been told more than once that I'm a natural at it. I think that leadership is distinct from people management, so thanks for giving it a separate category. There is strategy involved in leadership, and style – philosophy, even. Not everyone likes it and not everyone finds it easy." "And you do …?" Her tone was aloof,

bordering on ironic. He'd got the ball rolling – good! "As a matter of fact, yes, I always have. Back at Yale, I used to lead a student group; we wrote the local science newsletter. Also, the chess team …" Diane fussed in her chair slightly and David noticed that. He knew that Yale and chess irritated some people in the office and was glad he'd found a chance to mention both. These were objective assets, and he was not going to dumb himself down just to keep Diane comfortable. It worked. She interrupted him for the second time: "Well, yes, you see – this is exactly where we differ in our assessments." "'We' as in … yourself and Milena?" "As in, I and the company leadership … the real leaders, David." "Oh?" "Yes, 'we' thought you aren't exactly leadership material. The fit is sub-optimal, and it reflects onto your team's performance. In fact, the last budget showed …" "Give me a second, Diane, to digest this. That's helpful feedback, by the way. However, we both know Laurent does not break down outcomes by individual teams. He could have, however, pulled the data for various accounts, which of course are client-based. We Quants work on several of these accounts, as do a bunch of other teams – the traders, Sales, IT, technical writers. I'm sure all of this is common knowledge – even someone junior like Milena would know the SOPs." "Actually, the guidelines have been revised as of this year, and we have new performance indicators that show you guys specifically lagging behind the other teams. It's all there and we will share it very soon, at the next company meeting." "Will the re-structuring be announced then, too?" "Re-structuring? I have no idea what you're talking about. And, um, I am not sure I like your tone, David. The point of this meeting today is to let you know it isn't working. *You* are not working. In fact, I can see you know this already. You gave yourself a 7, an 8 … these are not grades fit for a team leader."

"Grades? I was not aware we are still in school, Diane. These are real-life scores assessing real-life situations. If anything, they show maturity … humbleness, one may call it. I'm not somebody with an exaggerated sense of his own value. What I am, and what I can be moving forward, is a pretty good leader – not an expert on every side of the business, but someone who inspires people to come together for a goal." "Yeah, well … I'm sorry you feel this way, David." Wow, this was out of context! "I'm sorry you feel this way" was Diane's go-to sentence, undoubtedly extracted from their HR bible. She normally used it well, feigning empathy with good effects, but this time she had missed the mark completely. He was not *feeling* in any way – he was *thinking*, engaging his pre-frontal cortex as Rada used to put it, giving Diane arguments and inviting her to think as well. He was doing exactly what he had not been allowed to do that fateful day in the office two years ago, after Clarissa and her letter to HR. Clearly, Diane had not been counting on this development. In fact, if what Rory had told him about the rumour mill was right, she might have counted on touching an old wound. Instead, she found a scar. Not much emotion to be excavated today – sorry, Diane! "We can debate it forever," she proceeded, with a quick glance to her watch, "but, as I said, we wanted to communicate that we will not be moving forward. You have not passed your probation, David. I'm sorry you feel … I mean, I'm sorry. That doesn't mean you cannot find a better fit somewhere else. Here is the letter of dismissal, dated today."

David made an extra effort to de-tense his shoulders as he reclined back in his chair, away from the table. This left Diane with her arm stretched in the air for a second. She eventually placed the envelope on the table and stared at him with muted eyes. David's chair squeaked a little, filling the awkward silence. "But I did. I did pass my probation. As of January 5th." "Why, we both know that appointment never took place!" "Well, that was the official appointment … with you and Andrei, I believe? Or perhaps you mean you and Milena – we don't seem to agree on who does what today. But I remember there were precisely two participants other than me – should we fact-check this real quick?" Diane kept quiet; her look was now piercing, saying: "All right, I know you know; drop the BS and get to the point." At least she'd stopped the niceness altogether. She'd also stopped checking her watch. David continued, trying his best to stay composed: "But then again, let's not bother with this now … it must have been a glitch. The Calendar system playing up, that kind of thing. What is important" – he raised his voice a little here – "is that Andrei called to tell me I could work from home. At 9 AM sharp, on Monday. Remember, we were all snowed under for a whole week? And when I asked about my probation, he said that all was fine and finished the call wishing me a Happy New Year." David was bluffing, but Diane's glazed eyes were showing him she'd stopped following the conversation. In a bid to buy herself some time, she gave another tone-deaf reply: "None of this makes sense. There was no probation review; period." "Well, you did schedule it. And then, after more than a week, you cancelled it – which means you or Andrei, or both, had nothing to comment on. In fact, you titled our second appointment – today's – 'performance assessment'. The first was called 'probation review'. Another glitch in the system? Or were you following Andrei's recommendation? If so –

and that would be my guess – he was… strategic, shall we say? Now he is perfectly covered, and you are left doing the less savoury job for him. So yeah, my first 6 months have elapsed and, according to my contract and the employment law, I am not on probation anymore. I've passed. And incidentally, I had a little chat with my solicitor last week; we were sorting out other issues related to my work visa and such. He advised that, at this point in time, I can claim unfair dismissal – and I might. On a number of grounds. One: you guys kept me in the dark about the supposed poor performance of my team, not giving me any chance to improve the 'situation'. Two: you did not make the new performance data available company-wide – if that data really does exist. And three: if it does, the data must have been produced by Laurent alone, without approval from up-top, which makes it void. Seamus is in New York and will be for some time. Andrei is not allowed to act on his behalf or sign off budgets. He can, however, sign the deal; you know, for the New York quants to take over. The pricing model is ready-made by them; all it needs is validation. Logically, for us the London quants, this means we'll be re-structured. Either merged with the New York group or, more realistically in the current climate, … dissolved. That would make business sense, wouldn't it?" No answer. "Thank you for listening, Diane. Oh, come to think of it, there is a fourth point: this dismissal letter was issued out of the blue. Normally, there have to be at least two prior written warnings. It's all in the company book – check with Milena. In fact, over the past month, I couldn't help but notice you guys systematically failing to be process-compliant. All kinds of bits and pieces that do not add together. Point being, you are entering the territory of wrongful termination. You don't want to be doing that, do you?"

David stopped, waiting. He felt instinctively it was time to be quiet. Past this point, it was no longer a game of tactics. As always when dealing with real people and their predictable unpredictability, it had become a gamble. But, if he was going to play roulette with his future, he might at least control the spin. And to do that, restraint was more effective in the moment. His mouth was dry, and he felt tiny drops of sweat trickling down his chest under his winter jacket. Never mind; Diane could not see any of that. Besides, she wasn't paying the usual attention to his reactions. She looked preoccupied, undecided. She stared at the dismissal letter, which was laying on the table in its envelope, untouched. "I'll be damned if I ever read one line of that letter!" David told himself. "I've got to keep my eyes on the game. The Pawn. The Pawn knows that, on the surface, the game is stacked against him. It's all about the bigger pieces with their grand, committal moves. But in the endgame, he is vital. Small, measured gains, and timely captures – that's how the Pawn will live to fight another day."

"What is it you want, David?" He was in luck – she had blinked first! David perked up. They'd finally come to the part he had rehearsed – ten times last night. "I am willing to resign; I will not stay if I'm not really wanted. And, since I am a permanent staff now, and in a senior position, I will work the required 3 months' notice. My severance package covers 6 months, as per my contract. So, 9 months in total. I'll gladly sign the non-compete agreement. In fact, I may not stick around in Finance for much longer, so you don't need to worry about potential competitors. I will not mention what you guys plan to do with us Quants, inside or outside my team. Should Laurent share the new performance data, and should my people ask how come our team is in the red but we were never told any of that, I'll say … I'll say there must have been a glitch. Laurent's been working from home a lot lately. Either that, or he's been hiding on the Strategy floor, sometimes in Andrei's office. And always using his personal laptop. By the way, you may want to check that too, Diane. It is company policy, not to mention Financial Conduct Authority rule, that all confidential data on investments and trades be stored on company computers. In their time scramble, Laurent and Andrei have overlooked this little detail." Diane was frozen in place. The Pawn had delivered check and mate.

By the time his meeting with Diane had finished, the floor was empty. Almost empty … there was Rory at his desk. This time, Rory didn't pay David the usual attention; he was busy. Chatting to him, half seated on the edge of his desk, was a female silhouette. She turned around and stood up at the sound of David passing. He was surprised to recognise Bogdana's exquisite features, a bit flushed. Hmm … not his business; he was the Pawn. A triumphant Pawn, at that. Out in the hall, he called the elevator but had no patience for it. He rushed down the stairs like a schoolboy at break time. And, like a boy, he gave out a big sigh – his loudest ever.

It was over – he was out! He'd broken free, taking with him the spoils of war. This was no small severance package: converted in Canadian dollars, 9 months of a team leader's pay was the deposit for a nice-looking condo in Montréal. No, not in Plamondon – he could do better! – but close enough to home. Time to take up Codrin on chess coaching at his CEGEP. This was one game David was proud to teach, one in which winning did not mean harming others. And, knowing himself, leadership would soon follow. All the while in London, he had been *en passant* – a passer-by who just happened to make a good capture. Not 'happened' – he should give himself some credit; plus, he had allies. Now it was time to cross the finish line and make the one true comeback. Back home, to Mum, to Dina's father who was pining for her. Time to allow them to be the grandparents they wished to be. What about Dina? She would have to listen to him for once. He'd had good reasons to rock the boat, lest the two of them should sink together. No need to "show them" anything, darling Dina. One cannot build a comeback using the same faulty blueprint twice. And even if one could, the world won't wait agape for this grand gesture of retribution. Life was not one cinematic chain reaction; it was a sum of well-considered moves, rarely spectacular and only slightly incremental. They'll have an argument, he and Dina; a big, loud one. But David knew by now that arguments were not the end of the world. Not when the alternative was to keep quiet, suppressed and secretive for years.

Speaking of secrets … he'd promised Diane not to utter a word about what had transpired in their meeting. Company rules … company ethics. Naturally, the ethics were meant for a subset of the employees – those unspecial and easily deceived – starting with himself, it would seem. Though he was mentally checking out of the office already, David could not help thinking of all the people he would have to deceive for another three months. He thought of Murray – how soon could he find another job at 58 years of age in this depressed market? Would Murray ever get to buy that retirement property he and his wife day-dreamed about? Well, not his problem anymore … cue Rory on the chess board. Rory the undeceivable. Rory, for whom winning the match was a far greater delight than playing the game. The boy who never talked about his childhood and who needed to be taught the basic human rules about not hurting others for sport. As he was making his way to the underground station, he texted Rory one last time: "Keep an eye on Laurent and his laptop. He is your true match. Stupid empath signing off."

And finally, Clarissa – would he ever get to close that chapter? He might not. Clarissa fancied herself to be the quintessential romantic. In this role, she had become adept at denying people a sense of closure. Not all people, of course; just those, like David, who saw something different in her. She wished to stay imprinted forever in the memory of her real or imaginary lovers. Not necessarily with a malicious intent; perhaps she was a natural at the game of Fata Morgana – the endless mirage, chased for a lifetime, intangible and thus unverifiable against reality. A natural indeed – just as *he* was at chess. "To each our own gifts in life … which means I'll have to bring about my own closure," David reasoned. "In the grand scheme of things, Clarissa is not so different from Rory – strange as it sounds. She's more confused, for sure, not as lucid. But, for both of them, love – however they conceive it – shows up as aggression. Except that Rory has got help in sorting out one from the other. Otherwise, at their core, they both have a profoundly distrustful, misanthropic side. Distilled down, their love is an attempt to dominate the 'other' as a way to make sure they never get submerged under their own feelings. They might have been one of those smart children who resisted the second marshmallow, but they must have made for lousy playground mates!"

And still … one question was lingering in David's mind, evading his attempts at closure. "Why did Clarissa bring me here, straight in the lions' den, for a second time? Why did she recommend me for the job? Was it purely machiavellic, their whole strategy of finding a fall guy – the King – and planting him on the board early enough so no one would suspect? Did they already know, she and Laurent, how things were going to pan out six months down the line? They couldn't have, not in the current economic chaos. At least *she* couldn't have – she doesn't have that kind of cool head on her shoulders. She has a special gift though: an uncanny intuition. I remember the first time we met; she gave me a warm smile and said something like: 'You'll do fine here, David – but it will take a while. British people do not wear their heart on their sleeve; they're cautious about who they let in, but, once they've made up their mind about you, you have in them a friend forever.' That was exactly what I wanted then: to be given the chance to prove myself and, ultimately, be accepted. I got the feeling she saw right through me. It was this instant rapport that made me feel at ease, disclose more and more about myself as time went by. I ended up giving her lots of ammunition – and lots of second chances. She must have known deep down that such a connection would be hard to destroy, despite the incident in Sloane Square, despite her letter and her atrocious betrayal. Funny thing is, I think she too felt the connection in all its strength. She couldn't let go of me either – or rather, of her fantasy about this young man with a vaguely French accent, mild-mannered, and rather nice-looking – so similar and yet so different from the men she'd met in London. And, for my part, what did I do? I fell right into it, move after move. With one small caveat: the second time around, I was not alone. Dina and I were together in a very real way. Surely even Fata Morgana knows, like we all do, that, at this stage in our life, sex is the ultimate deal-breaker. When you have climaxed, the out-of-reach fantasy of the perfect lover has a way of dissipating instantly under the overwhelming power of hormones and the human imperative for love and reproduction. Clarissa had never had a hold on me that way; so, she had to test the strength of our bond once more. She did it the only way she knew: through another betrayal. Why did she want me back? I'm guessing to swipe clean her past of litigious affairs, dramatic twists of fate and imagined persecutions, and start fresh: a new and improved Clarissa. Clarissa 2.0 – or, judging by her dossier with Larry, 4.0 – who would finally be able to hold on to a good man and do no harm if unprovoked. An ordinary Clarissa living an ordinary, if less passionate, relationship. By giving me a second chance, she was actually giving herself one. Was I not right about her and Rory? Theirs is a selfish kind of love – and, soon enough, it turns dangerous under the pressure of their own inner turmoil. So, here I am, the object of Rory's fascination and of Clarissa's repeated attempts at normality. She *had* to call me back – just as she's keen to deny closure in others, she is obsessed with finding it herself."

***

The time was only five o'clock. That one hour with Diane had felt like ages. David was drained but tense and restless. Outside, the air was cool and fresh. He breathed it deep into his lungs to cleanse away the heavy, stuffy atmosphere of the meeting room. He called Dina to ask if she'd got home. Her voice was ebullient on the other side:

"It's happened! The baby special – we're having it tonight. They've asked me for suggestions and now we're all at 'Maple Leaf' in Covent Garden, watching ice hockey and waiting for poutine. I managed to get them excited about Canadian junk food!" "Sounds like you guys are having fun!" David replied quickly, trying to match her tone. He was somewhat relieved. Dina was bound to come back in high spirits after the girls' night out – this might just take the edge off what was about to happen between them. "What shall I do with myself tonight?" he wondered. The last thing he wanted was to go back to an empty apartment – he'd had enough of that last time he lost his job. Reflexively, he took the Jubilee line and got off at Canary Wharf, facing a sea of commuters going in all directions. This time, he made his way with ease.

No longer trapped within his narrow slice of the event-horizon, no longer shaking under the fear of future, David felt unfettered, light, open to the unknown. Getting lost amongst the crowd was not enough tonight. For the first time in months, the city looked boundless and inviting in front of him. He picked up the pace and rushed along the riverbank, elbowing the few disoriented passers-by who found themselves in his way. The profile of Canary Wharf, with its slick buildings – mostly banks – was now behind him. Somewhere out there was his room – a tiny light against the darkening sky. That room was his no more; Saul was its rightful owner. Right now, he must have looked like one the runners back home in Plamondon Park, the ones he called 'the maniacs'. He charged ahead, faster, as fast as he could, until he was out breath. Then he stopped, panting, breathing the familiar damp air of the docks mixed with the salty scent of algae. A few drops of sweat burrowed themselves in his brows.

It was the good kind of sweat, not the anxious drip running down his chest during the meeting with Diane. The energy of the evening was palpable, and his restlessness had not gone away yet. What next?

Then he remembered: the Dalí exhibition was still on at Southbank Centre. Delphine thought it was worth seeing. If he crossed Tower Bridge, he might still make it before closing time. David carried on running, purposefully now, until he heard the Big Ben striking seven in the distance. Nearly there! As he entered the centre, he realised he must have looked a mess – the typical London commuter. Hmm … only on the outside; inside, he felt relaxed and peaceful. "I am ok. I'm ready – what for, I am not sure." A few sculptures were placed at the entrance, like guardians to this quirky universe. David passed them quickly, making a mental note to come back later if there was time. He'd just noticed the "Spellbound" corner: Dalí's magnificent painting next to the dream sequence from the film.

He sprinted to the "Spellbound" display as if attracted by a magnet. David remembered the dream scene very well, as he remembered everything concerning dreams. He appraised the work with a critical eye – after all, he knew a thing or two about dreaming. David thought Hitchcock had overdone it: the whole connection with psychoanalysis and the subconscious mind seemed slightly forced. But how to make a point about such an esoteric topic at the time? You bring along a madman artist like Dalí, that's how – someone so conversant with the world of fantasy that he lived inside it most of the time. Perhaps Dalí had a point here. Perhaps the mystics have a point too, perceiving the so-called "real world" as a feeble projection. David took turns watching the painting, then the film, over and over, hypnotised. "To dream … sometimes, a dream is all it takes. Not as in day-dreaming: that's escapism, retreat in the face of conflicts, of life. A different kind of dream: a sign, a way to build a bridge". In "Spellbound", the bridge got built from within, with the help of a therapist, allowing the character to heal the fractures of his mind. For David and his mother, dreams were a nod from the outside – a higher plane. But still a bridge to deeper understanding.

"We spend our days walking around like shadows, projected on a screen by an eccentric artist – someone we'll never know. As soon as we wake up, the spirit of our dreams is all but banished from awareness. We think we choose our actions willingly, but we are at the mercy of our scripts and games. We manufacture a tyranny of logic to keep us trapped in one dimension. We think we learn from observations, interactions … we think there is a science to our life. When really, we are disconnected. We lack resilience because we lack fluidity: when under stress, our minds split and fracture like the dry, brittle structures they've become. What we should do is learn to heed our dreams: they are the rivers of our mind. If they don't get submerged under our constant chatter, they'll bring a sense of knowing beyond the world of words and facts. As for myself, I've made a promise back in Benny Park, that I will watch the sky more often. And if I do, one day a speck of stardust will drop into my dreams … and with it, a vision meant for me only. After all, *she* chose to name me David."

Editor's Note – En Passant

En Passant struck and engaged me on many levels. The novel tackles the complex theme of the 2008 financial crisis through a deeply human lens, skilfully blending the historical and economic dimension with the intimate and existential journey of the protagonist, David.

From the very first pages, the reader is drawn into the collapse not only of the banks, but also of David's personal certainties: the loss of his job, the dramatic episode with Clarissa, and the sudden social isolation. The scene where Clarissa falsely accuses him and he becomes the office scapegoat was particularly powerful to me, because it encapsulates the sense of bewilderment and betrayal that accompanies the protagonist throughout the first part of the story.

The section set in Montréal adds new depth to the character: the return to his family, the protective love of his parents, and the sleepless nights filled with grief mark an important passage from trauma to the search for healing. I especially appreciated the way the writer interweaves childhood memories, dreams, and philosophical reflections: small flashes of spirituality that lighten the weight of David's lived experience.

The relationship with Dina, on the other hand, introduces a dimension that is both luminous and fragile. The seesaw scene in the park, where both characters' hidden wounds are revealed, was one of the moments that moved me the most: it conveys that the novel is not only about financial crises, but also about relational fragility and rebuilding trust. The intimate and everyday moments with Dina, narrated with naturalness and delicacy, make the story extremely true and relatable.

I also found the chapters dedicated to Clive and Rory particularly stimulating, as they provide David with new keys to interpret the world: from philosophy to technology, from psychology to ethical issues. It feels as if each character represents a piece in the protagonist's path toward inner rebirth.

In conclusion, I found *En Passant* to be a rich and multi-layered novel, able to alternate pain and hope, rationality and spirituality, introspection and social dialogue. The metaphor of chess, which accompanies David until the very end, becomes the perfect key: it is not only about finding the winning move, but also about understanding when it is necessary to redefine the rules of the game.

--

Ginevra Grasso

EUROPE BOOKS

europe books